LAUREL-LEAF
BOOKS

It was the first thing I saw when I went into the bathroom. It was dark brown and it was wrapped around the bristles—woven actually, in and out and around.

I heard my father leaving for work. I grabbed the brush and ran downstairs. "Daddy! Daddy! He did it again! That pig did it again!" I caught up to him halfway down the driveway. He turned and looked me up and down—mostly down—and gave me that smirky well-well-what-have-we-here look he uses when I'm doing something a little crazy. Like standing in the middle of the driveway early on a Saturday morning in my Wayne Gretzky nightshirt and bare feet with a toothbrush in my hand.

I jabbed the toothbrush at him. "Look!"

Still the smirky grin. "I'm looking, believe me."

"Stop it, Daddy. Here. The toothbrush."

"You trying to tell me I have bad breath?"

"Daddy, look!" I nearly mashed it into his eye. *"Look!"*

He recoiled, squinted. "Ah—yes. What *is* that?"

I stamped on the asphalt. "It's a hair!"

JERRY SPINELLI's first novel for young readers, *Space Station Seventh Grade,* is available in a Dell Laurel-Leaf edition. He lives in Havertown, Pennsylvania.

Who Put That Hair in My Toothbrush?

Jerry Spinelli

LAUREL-LEAF BOOKS

Published by
Dell Publishing
a division of .
Bantam Doubleday Dell Publishing Group, Inc.
666 Fifth Avenue
New York, New York 10103

ISBN: 0-440-99485-3

RL: 5.7

Reprinted by arrangement with Little, Brown and Company, Inc.

Printed in the United States of America

April 1986

10   9   8   7

RAD

For Muffin,
who helped me write this book
and my life

Megin

THE SADDEST SHOWER of all is the one you take the night before school starts in September. It's like you're not just washing the day's dirt away, you're washing the whole summer down the drain — all the fun, all the long, free days. So it's sad. So the last thing I needed, taking my end-of-summer shower, was something to make it even worse. But that's exactly what I got.

It started while I was washing my hair: someone flushed the toilet and the shower water turned scalding hot. "Toddie!" I yelled, scooting on my heels to the other end of the tub. My little brother is the only one who goes to the bathroom while I'm taking a shower. I peeked around the curtain. No Toddie. No anybody. But the door was open. "Shut the door!" I yelled. The door slammed shut.

I figured that would be it. Wrong. A couple minutes later, just as I got all soaped up, the water changed again, this time to freezing. I jumped back — and rammed my hip into the soap dish — pain! I peeked out, massaging my hip. Steaming hot water was gushing from the faucet in the

3

sink. Again: nobody there, the door open. I knew right then who was behind it all.

"Shut the door!" I yelled. The door stayed open. I had to get the door shut and the sink water off. They were both too far to reach from the tub. I pushed the curtain outside the tub, then I stepped out onto the floor with the curtain still in front of me. Dripping. Hip killing me. Door still a long way off. I inched away from the tub. I was getting closer, but with every inch, more and more of me was sticking out from behind the curtain. Pretty soon the only thing covering me was the red plastic triangle of the curtain's lower corner. I reached out my leg as far as it would go; my big toe wiggled way short of the door.

Only one thing to do. I dashed for the door, leaving the curtain behind. Right then, in mid-dash, is when things really started happening fast: suddenly Toddie was standing — gawking — in the doorway; I froze; I screamed; I dashed back to the curtain; I banged my leg against the toilet; I wrapped myself in the curtain; the curtain, like a machine gun, came pop-pop-popping off the rod; I screamed again —

"YYYAAAAAAAAAAAAAAAAAAAAAAAAAHHH!"

Then my father came rushing in. He saw the shower running in the bathtub, he saw the water boiling into the sink, he saw his daughter, wrapped in the shower curtain, dripping and screaming in the middle of the bathroom — and what did he say? "Hey, your dimples don't show when you're screaming."

I screamed louder.

He turned off the sink water and the shower. "Okay, okay, Dimpus. Now what's going on?"

"I'll kill him," I swore.

He looked around, pretending not to know what I was talking about. "Kill? Who?"

"You know who."

He rubbed his chin and pretended to think. "Hmm, let's see now. You said 'him.' So it's a 'he' you're going to kill. Can't be me. That leaves two other 'hes' in the house." He turned to Toddie, who was still standing goo-goo-eyed in the doorway. "You're not going to kill your little brother, are you, Megin?"

"Daddy," I said, "he's making Toddie do stuff to me. He made him flush the toilet and turn the water on."

"Toddie," my father said gently, "did somebody make you do that?"

Toddie stuck out his chest. "Nobody make me do nuffin'."

"Daddy, he probably paid him off. He pays him to torture me. Look in his pockets. Go ahead — *look.*" My father reached into Toddie's pockets and pulled out two nickels. "See!" I screeched.

"Megin," he said, "you can't convict somebody on two nickels. That's not proof."

My hip and my leg were killing me and I felt like I was being swallowed by a giant fish, and he was talking about proof. Still drenched, I stormed out of the bathroom and over to Grosso's room. I could hear barbells clanking inside. His door was locked. I started kicking it and banging and screaming. "I'll kill him! I'll kill him!" By the time my father dragged me back to the bathroom, my feet and fists were sore too.

But I wasn't about to give up. I slipped from the shower curtain into a towel and had my father put the curtain back up. Then I made him stand guard outside the door while I went on with my shower. Sure enough, in about a minute the water changed again, to ice. I screamed. I could hear my father tearing downstairs. When he came back, he looked sheepish. "Sorry, Dimpus," he said, "Mommy started the washer."

Greg

"... forty-eight ... forty-nine ... *fifty*."

Done. I was ready. If she was ever going to notice me, this would be the day.

Suddenly I was nervous. Terrified. *God, this is it!* What if she *still* didn't notice me? What if I still looked the same? What if those million sit-ups went to waste? What if she met somebody down the shore over the summer? What if ...

Stay calm, stay calm. I sat on the edge of my bed and started taking long, deep breaths. *Relax, relax.* Ever since school had ended in June, I had had only one goal in life: to make myself good-looking enough so Jennifer Wade would have to notice me. I got subscriptions to *Muscles* and *Body Beautiful.* I exercised and lifted weights. I covered myself with Coppertone and tanned in the sun. I used Sassoon shampoo and Sassoon conditioner and Sassoon rinse, and I brushed my teeth with Close-up at least four times every

day. I drank Pro/Gain and I ate tons of eggs and raw vegetables and fruit and red meats. Plus potato skins. I read
they're good for the complexion.

And now it was time. One final first-day-of-school series
of curls (25 each arm), push-ups (50) and sit-ups (50),
and the job was done. I went to the bathroom and checked
out my summer's work. I was re-created. A new kid. A sort
of Sassoon–Pro/Gain–Coppertone Frankenkid.

But I still felt the same inside.

I washed my face but couldn't find a towel. I was ticked.
I hauled my wet face right into Megamouth's room. There
they were: one towel wrapped around her head, one on a
chair, two on the floor.

"Dad-dee! Dad-dee! Greg's in my room! Get outta my
room!"

I grabbed the towel on the chair and got out. I felt something hit me in the back.

"Somebody better do something about that room of
hers," I told my parents in the kitchen. "We're gonna get
roaches."

"You know," my father said, "it amazes me that two
children in the same family can be so different. One so
neat, one so sloppy."

"Doesn't amaze me," said my mother. "Greg, pancakes?"

"No thanks."

"Not even on the first day of school? I don't do this all
the time, you know."

"No thanks."

Megamouth came in mocking. "No thannnks, no
thannnks. He doesn't want to junk up that beautiful body
of his."

"Once you get roaches, you know, you can't get rid of them."

"Greg, you're going to have more than that milk shake, aren't you?"

"It's not milk shake. It's Pro/Gain."

"If you don't want the pancakes I got up early to make you, then what?"

Megamouth swooned. "Oh, Jennifer, my darling, I love you, I adore you."

"Greg, I'm waiting for your order. I only do this one day a year, you know. Now what'll it be?"

"A grapefruit. Y'know, roaches've been around since before the dinosaurs."

Megamouth made a smooching sound. "Oh, Jennifer, I'm wild about you! I simply went crazy without you all summer!"

She kept interrupting like that, but I ignored her. "They hang around where there's food and darkness," I said. "Just what's in that room."

"Why, Jennifer, don't you recognize me? It's Greg. Greg Tofer."

"If somebody comes in here and sees that room, they could sic the Board of Health on us."

"That's right! Remember ugly old Greg Tofer?"

"I read this article — once you get roaches, you might never get rid of them."

"Since you saw me last, I lifted my dumbbells and I shampooed with my Sassoon and I drank my proteins and now look at me — I'm *gorgeous!*"

"Never."

"Even my zits are smaller!"

My father stood up — as usual, this big grin on his face. "Well, family, I'm off to support you now. Don't forget: Help your father — push somebody into the mud."

He always says that. He's an appliance salesman at Sears, and one of the things he sells is washing machines.

I finished my grapefruit, grabbed a potato skin from the refrigerator (my mother saves them for me), and took off.

You might have thought just a weekend had passed, not a whole summer. As usual, Old Mrs. Greeley next door was sweeping off her sidewalk. (You could *eat* off her sidewalk.) Valducci was waiting at the first corner, Poff at the second. Just like always.

But everything wasn't the same.

Valducci jumped out in front, whirled, and did a high-kick in our faces that stopped us cold. Valducci is into karate or something. "Hey, baby! We are now" — an open hand snapped down to split an invisible cinder block — "*chakkah!* — ninth-graders!"

"Big rip," said Poff, who is built like a *visible* cinder block.

Fast as a lizard's tongue, Valducci's hands flicked out, tattooed Poff's head up one side and down the other, then shot back before Poff could raise a hand. Valducci's quick, you have to give him that. "Ninth grade, man! We're gonna rule that school!" Valducci went kicking and jerking and chopping ahead of us. "We are — sokka! — kings now, babeee — Look out — sokka! — teachers — look out — sokka! — everybodeee — Gonna rule — sokka! — that — sokka! — school — sokka sokka *Chakkalahhh!*"

Valducci was right, even if he did get a little carried away. No longer were we seventh-grade zeroes or eighth-grade halfways. Suddenly I felt a little bigger in the world. I grinned. "Yeah, right, ninth-graders now."

"Big rip," said Poff.

Coming up to the school, I only had one question: Where was Jennifer Wade? I couldn't go obviously gawking around after her; nobody in ninth grade knew about my thing for her, not even Poff and Valducci, and I wanted to keep it that way. So, while the outside of me was slapping hands and saying "How was your summer?" the inside of me was like a sack of blinded eyes.

A couple times I saw girlfriends of hers, once I thought I heard her voice, but by the time the door opened, I still hadn't spotted her. I was almost relieved. I didn't know what I'd do if I saw her, anyway. The whole idea was to have *her* see *me*. All summer long I had been directing this little movie in my head:

SCENE I

Time: First day of school.
Place: Avon Oaks Junior High.
* Somewhere in the hallway.*

JENNIFER. Hi, Greg.
ME. Hi, Jen.
JENNIFER. Gee, you look great.
ME. Thanks. You're looking pretty good yourself.
JENNIFER [*blushing*]. Thank you.
ME. My pleasure.
JENNIFER. Say, Greg, that's a great tan you have.
ME. Thanks. You have a pretty good one too.
JENNIFER [*blushing*]. Thank you.
ME. My pleasure.
JENNIFER. You weren't down the beach all summer
        by any chance, were you?
ME. Nah. I just love the outdoors, that's all.

JENNIFER. Well, that golden tan really sets off your eyes nice.

ME. Thanks. So does yours.

JENNIFER [*blushing*]. Thank you.

ME. My pleasure.

JENNIFER. And your forearms, I can't help noticing them. They seem so strong, so rugged. And wow — look — look at that vein running down there, how it's popping out!

ME. Yeah.

JENNIFER. That's really great.

ME. Thanks, Jen.

SCENE II

Time: Next day.
Place: Same.

JENNIFER. Hi, Greg.

ME. Hi, Jen.

JENNIFER. How's school going?

ME. Pretty good, thanks.

JENNIFER [*shyly*]. Say, Greg, do you mind if I ask you something?

ME. Not at all.

JENNIFER [*adorably*]. Well, I'm having a party Saturday night, and I was wondering if you'd like to come — with me, of course.

ME. Mm . . . okay. Sure, Jen. Sounds good.

JENNIFER [*excitedly*]. Oh wow! Great!

Not for one second did I stop squeezing the little rubber ball in my hand. I swore no matter where or when I met her, my forearm vein was going to be humping out. Like a python on a sidewalk.

She wasn't in any of my morning classes, and I didn't see her in the hallways. When I couldn't spot her in the lunchroom, I really started to worry. Afternoon: still no Jennifer.

At the bell I rushed outside and hung around bus No. 4, the one she always took. I saw every person who got on, saw the bus take off, without her. Squeezing the rubber ball like mad, I ran back inside, to the office.

The secretary looked up. "Yes?"

"Uh — it's not important, just wondering about something."

"What is it?"

"Uh — a student, ninth-grader, I think. A girl."

"What about her?"

"Well — uh — ah never mind —"

I bolted from the office, my face on fire. I couldn't do it. But I had to. Couldn't. Had to. Suddenly, coming toward me in the dusky hallway, one of her friends. We passed. I turned, kept walking backward, called, breezily, "Hey — Karen."

She turned. "Hi."

"You — uh — still friends with that girl? What's her name? Jennifer something?"

"Wade?"

"Yeah, that's it."

"What about her?"

We were still backing away from each other, so we were practically shouting by now. "Didn't see her today!"

"I know!"

"She sick?"

"She moved!"

"What?"

"Moved! To Conestoga!"

I breezed on out the door, nonchalanted it down the steps, whistled a football fight song, cooled it all the way out to the curb, where the last bus was leaving. I stood right behind it and let its gas-fart smother me; then I wound up, and with all the summer and strength in my arm, I fired the rubber ball. It hit right where a bug-eyed seventh-grader had his stupid nose mashed against the back window.

Megin

I THOUGHT Sue Ann was going to pee herself, she was so excited.

"D'jah hear about the girl from California?"

"From where?"

"California!"

"What about her?"

"She's here!"

"Who?"

"The girl from California!"

"So?"

"Didn't you hear about her?"

"Sue Ann, we just started junior high school an hour ago."

"I know, but everybody's talking about her already."

"What about her?"

"I don't know, all kinds of stuff. They said she's really something."

"Yeah?"

"Yeah. *Really* something."

The girl from California — that's all I heard about. Every five minutes Sue Ann came rushing up with a new report: "She wears silver sandals!" "An anklet!" "*Two* anklets!" "Green toenail polish!" "Green eye shadow!" "Big hoop earrings!" "Her name's Zoe!"

"*Zoe?*" I screeched.

"Yeah. Can you believe it?"

"Zoe?"

"Yeah, Zoe."

"Nobody's name is *Zoe.*"

"Megin" — she squeezed my arm — "she's from Cali-*for*-nia."

Well, I never saw her the first day. She wasn't in any of my classes, and I guess she wasn't in my lunch shift either. On the second day, coming to school, Sue Ann pointed to a crowd near the door.

"She's in there."

"Who?"

"The girl from California."

"How do you know?"

"I just know. She's in there. Go ahead, take a look."

She was pushing me.

"Sue Ann! Knock it off! I gotta lotta things to do around here without having to listen to you jabber all the time about some weirdo from California. Now, are you going out for lacrosse with me or not?"

Suddenly she was yanking me around. "Look, Megin! There she is! Look!"

"Oh cripes." I smacked her hand away. "You're disgusting." I marched into school and absolutely refused to look.

Best friend or no best friend, Sue Ann can be a pain sometimes. She gets so — I don't know — flighty, hyper. I didn't have time to be bothered. By the end of the day, I

16

had signed up for stage crew and lacrosse. I picked lacrosse because it's the closest thing to ice hockey, which is my all-time favorite sport. In lacrosse you get a stick with this fishnet pocket in it to carry and pass around a hard rubber ball. I was only on the field a minute before the coach came blaring her whistle.

"Hey! You!"

"Huh?"

"What's your name?"

"Megin."

"Megin who?"

"Tofer."

"What do you think you're doing, Tofer?"

"Playing lacrosse."

"What exactly did I tell you to do, Tofer?"

"Uh, practice carrying the ball?"

"On the stick? By yourself?"

"Yeah."

"Did I say anything about charging into somebody else and stealing her ball?"

I glanced at Sue Ann, who was wearing a big pout on her face. "No."

"Take a lap," the coach snapped and walked off. "With your ball and stick."

Sue Ann started to snicker. "Baby," I hissed at her.

The coach whirled. "What?"

"Nothing."

"*Two* laps."

Ten minutes into my first lacrosse practice and I was ready to quit. Bad enough that I had to take the laps, but every couple steps the ball would bounce out of the stick pocket. The first two or three times I just picked up the ball and put it back in the pocket. Then I heard the coach's voice booming across the field: "Scoop it with the stick, Tofer! *Scooop* it!"

"Scoop you," I whispered.

Next time the ball bounced out I tried to scoop it; instead I only knocked it farther away. When I finally caught up with it, I started beating it with the stick.

"*Three* laps, Tofer!"

Halfway through the third lap I was practically a cripple. Ice hockey was never like this. For the millionth time the ball bounced out; this time it hit my foot and went shooting off toward the sidewalk. I staggered after it, and next thing I knew I was tripping and falling flat on my face. I just lay there for a while, taking a rest and spitting out grass and waiting for boomer-voice to go, "*Four* laps, Tofer!" When I bothered to look for the ball, I saw it just a few feet away. There was a foot on it — a foot with a silver sandal, an anklet, green toenails. It was a long time before I looked up and finally, finally saw the girl from California.

Greg

> Set of weights. Almost new (used
> 2½ months). 10-lb. dumbbells.
> Can of Pro/Gain (unopened).
> Back issues of "Muscles" and
> "Body Beautiful." CHEAP.

I PUT the ad away and went downstairs to wait for my mom to come out of it. She looked dead on the sofa, her hands folded over her chest. I swear, every time I see her come out of it I think of a vampire rising out of a coffin.

I never believed in self-hypnosis until my mother actually learned it a couple of years ago. "If I don't, I'll never make it. I'm surviving" was what she said — whatever that means.

At first she said she was going to do it just for the summer, to "survive" having all us kids around all day. But when school started, she kept on doing it, every afternoon from 3:00 to 3:15. Now she "survives" till 3:30.

She came out of it at 3:30 on the dot. She didn't seem in any big hurry to get up. She just stared at the ceiling for a while, not even blinking. I felt like an intruder in a tomb. I cleared my throat to let her know I was there. Her head turned, her eyes were staring straight at me, but somehow I still wasn't sure she saw me.

"How do you get an ad in the *Tradin' Times*?" I asked her.

She blinked. "Phone it in, I guess."

I hung around. I wasn't ready to leave.

She noticed. "Greg?"

"Huh?"

"Something the matter?"

"No, why?"

"Okay, never mind."

Sometimes my mother infuriates me. Like, she never asks what's the matter twice. I figured I'd give her another chance. "Guess you noticed the Sassoon shampoo's gone."

"I'll get you more next time we shop."

"I don't mean that. I threw it out."

"Oh."

"Won't need it anymore."

"Okay."

"No-Frills'll be good enough."

"Okay."

Infuriating. Crazy mother. How many ninth-grade guys talk to their mothers about girl stuff? But this mother makes you want to. How? By not listening. And the more she doesn't listen, the more you want to tell her.

She got up and headed for the kitchen. *Okay, one last chance.* "What's for dinner?"

"Fish cakes."

"Guess I won't eat."

"Thought you like fish cakes."

"Lost my appetite."

"Okay."

"Just . . . lost it."

"Fine."

I gave up and went upstairs. I had to talk to somebody. *Had* to. But who? My mother was useless. Valducci? Forget Valducci. He could never shut up or stay still long enough to listen. How do you talk to a jackhammer? Poff? I could talk to him about some things — sports, bodyweight (hard stuff) — but not something like girls (soft stuff). Poff is the maturest guy I know. He's a man, really. Sometimes it startles me to see him heading into junior high school. Oh, Poff would listen, all right, and he might even say more than "Big rip," but behind his eyes he would be losing respect for me. Girls, love — Poff is above those things.

I even thought of Leo Borlock. A lot of kids — mostly girls, actually — go to him for advice. But just the thought of Poff catching me coming out of Leo's was enough to make me scratch that idea.

So what did I do? I took a shower, and as I looked up at the shower nozzle it seemed to say to me: *Let it all out, kid. I'm listening to ya.* "Y'know," I said, "it doesn't make things any better knowing she only moved over to Conestoga. Ten miles away might as well be Alaska, for all I can get there . . . And the crime of it is, I look a whole lot better than I did three months ago, when she saw me last." I posed for the nozzle. "Right? I mean, if she didn't like me before, she just *might* like me now, right? Because this is as good as I get . . .

"Okay, okay . . . so, say she saw me and she *still* didn't like me. Okay, fine, at least I would've had my shot, right? That's all I ever asked for. My shot. And the tragedy of it — want to hear the rock-bottom, cold-blooded, murderest tragedy of it? I'll tellya: she was starting to like me."

I decided to have dinner after all. Megamouth didn't shut up the whole time: "What happened to Jennifer Wade? . . . Heard she moved. . . . Where's the Sassoon? . . ."

"Megin, *enough*," my mother snapped.

"May-gin," my father sang across the table, "one of these days you're gonna have yourself a boyfriend, and what are you going to say if Greg teases you like this?"

"I don't care," Megamouth said, and went on: "Who are those skinny muscles gonna impress now? . . . Bet she's having a good time in Conestoga. . . . Lotsa cute boys over there in Conestoga."

Finally my mother had had enough. "Go, Megin. Upstairs. Leave the table."

Toddie cheered, but I was the one who stood up. "That's okay," I said. "She doesn't know what she's talking about. So happens I'm going out with Jennifer Wade" — I tapped my fork twice on the table — "Saturday night" — and I walked out.

Megin

SATURDAY NIGHT I stayed over at Sue Ann's. We lay in the dark with her TV on — the picture, not the sound. The only sound was our voices.

"So," she said, "when're you going to tell me what you think?"

"Think about what?"

"You know. *Her.*"

"What do you want me to say?"

"I don't know. Something. How can you see her and not say something?"

"I'm not."

"Well, you're *thinking* something. Tell me you're not."

"I'm not."

She hit me with her pillow and we both laughed.

"Tell me what *you* think," I said.

"I've been telling you all week long what I think."

"Uh-uh. You been telling me *things* about her. Facts. Not what you *think* about her."

She didn't answer. The TV was showing a commercial.

It looked funny without sound, this guy all happy and excited and hugging this lady. And then you saw why: she had gotten his shirt collar clean.

"Well?" I said.

Sue Ann reached over and took her good-luck monkey from me. "Well, I wonder if all the girls in California are like that."

"That's not thinking, that's wondering."

"You ever know anybody else from California?"

"I don't think so. Michigan once."

"That near California?"

"Don't think so."

"Megin?"

"Huh?"

"What *do* you think? About Californians, I mean. Are they all like that out there?"

"Nah."

"No? How do you know?"

"Some of them wear *blue* toenail polish."

We cracked up.

The silent TV was showing a lady in a body suit swinging on a high bar, then riding a horse, then playing tennis. Suddenly the screen was filled with this big box of Maxi Pads.

"Megin?"

"Huh?"

"You think they have virgins in California?"

"Of course they do, idiot. What about all the kindergarten girls out there?"

She grabbed her monkey back and started whipping on me. "I know! I know! I know!"

When the subject turns to sex, Sue Ann tends to get all

fascinated and giggly, even hysterical. Me, I get mostly bored or disgusted.

I grabbed a lashing monkey leg. "Sue Ann, I'm warning ya, I'll pull it off."

She let go. She was panting. "Okay — c'mon, Megin, you know what I mean. What do you think?"

"How should I know? Did you see me go to California to count the virgins?"

"I'm just asking."

"Anyway, *you* don't even know what a virgin is."

"Oh yeah?"

"Yeah."

"Yeah?"

"Okay" — I called her bluff — "tell me."

"You tell me."

"I asked you first."

"For me to know and you to find out."

"Right, Sue Ann. I'll bet you know. You don't even know what a lip lock is."

"A what?" she squeaked.

I started to howl.

She smashed a pillow into my face. "Quiet! My parents are asleep."

We shut up for a while and watched the TV. Then, with her face all ghosty in the tube glow, Sue Ann said, "Think Zoe is?"

I had been wondering myself, but hearing Sue Ann come out with it made the whole idea sound ridiculous. "Man, she's only in seventh grade."

"Yeah, but Megin" — she turned to me so that her face was half glow, half dark — "that girl might be *in* seventh grade, but she's no *seventh-grader*. Know what I mean?" I knew, and I didn't especially want to know, and I didn't especially want to keep talking about this. But Sue Ann wasn't ready to quit. "They mature faster in California, kids do."

"That so?"

"Yeah, they do."

"How do you know?"

"She said. Zoe."

"She spoke to you?"

"I sort of overheard."

"What are you anyway, her groupie?"

Sue Ann was on her knees in front of me now, like an excited puppy dog. "I couldn't hear what she was saying because I was too far back, y'know? But Chrissie Blalong and Jeannette O'Brien and Peggy Russo were in there close, and you should've seen their faces when she told them stuff."

"I'll bet you asked them what."

"I did! I did! I asked Peggy."

"You're gross."

"Megin," — she edged closer, whispering, "girls get their periods in fifth grade out there. Some even *fourth!*"

"Yeah?"

"Yeah."

"Nah."

"Yeah. No kiddin'. She's had her period for *years.*"

"Just what I always wanted to know." I reached out and flicked off the TV. "I'm going to sleep." I threw her monkey at her and lay down.

After about a minute, her voice came through the darkness. "And she worships Halley's comet."

"Who's what?"

"Halley's comet. You know, the big comet that's coming? We heard about it in school?"

"*Worships* it?"

"Yeah."

"A comet."

"Yeah, Halley's. She says it'll start being visible in the sky pretty soon, and then things are *really* gonna happen."

"That so."

"I don't mean *I* believe all that. I'm just saying about her."

"Good night."

" 'Night."

Sure enough, another minute and out of the darkness: "So what do you think *now*, Megin? About her being a virgin, huh? . . . huh? . . ."

I made my breathing loud and slow to pretend I was asleep.

Greg

CRAZY. Here it was, Saturday night, and I was leaving the house to go on a date I didn't really have with Jennifer Wade. I'd have to stay out date-late and make sure not to bump into any of my family. All because I let Megamouth badger me into lying.

When I met up with Poff and Valducci, I steered them away from the mall. I figured that was the one place where I might bump into Megamouth; plus, my father's Sears was there.

"So where?" said Valducci.

"How about the dollar movies?" I suggested.

"No way," said Poff.

"Why not?" I said. "What's playing?"

"*Bambi*."

"Hey!" piped Valducci, "sounds good. I hear the deer gets it. Maybe a high-kick to the Adam's apple." He hopped onto a stone wall in front of a lawn and high-kicked a dead twig from a tree. "*Chakkah! Bambi Meets Bruce Lee!*"

Poff just shook his head and kept walking.

We couldn't decide where to go, so we went to McDonald's to think it over. Must have been a bad night for making decisions — half the school was there.

"Let's eat in the parking lot," I suggested after we got our food.

"No way, José," said Valducci. "We gonna sit in style."

He dived into the mob, disappeared, and next thing we knew there was an earsplitting whistle and Valducci's hand waving above the heads. When we got to him, he was at a booth where two ninth-grade girls were sitting, Anita Liuto and Sara Bellamy. We all knew each other a little.

"Hey," went Valducci, "Anita and Sara just invited us to sit with them."

Obviously this was news to the girls. They shot *should-we* looks at each other, followed by *it's-okay-with-me-if-it's-okay-with-you* looks. A good thing, because Valducci had already slid in next to Anita. Which wasn't surprising. Anita is Italian (Valducci loves Italian girls), and she was the prettier one.

I saw what was coming. Right away I plopped down next to Valducci. He was in tight enough to Anita that I had more than half a butt of seat room. I hated to stick Poff with Sara Bellamy, but you know the old saying: All's fair in love, war, and booth-sitting.

In a way, I was thankful for Valducci. Without his mouth there would have been total silence at the table. He opened with "So, where you girls headin' for tonight?"

The girls said they didn't know. They had been thinking about the dollar movies, until they heard *Bambi* was playing.

Valducci got this shocked look on his face. "You mean you thought it was just *Bambi*? The plain old regular *Bambi*?"

The girls nodded, a little confused.

"Oh jeez." Valducci wagged his head and slapped the table; two french fries toppled from Anita's bag. "Didn't you know? It's a remake. Y'know, like they did a remake of *King Kong*?" The girls were shifting their eyes from him to each other. "Well, that's what they did with *Bambi*. It's the remake, not the old Walt Disney cartoon. They made this mechanical deer, y'know, like they made the shark in *Jaws*? Only this time the deer is the father, *Big* Bambi, and he's bigger than a moose, and he's really p-o'ed because Bambi Junior got shot. So he stalks the guys that did it all the way back to the city."

By now Anita was coming straight on with a dirty look, so Valducci laughed. "Okay, I was just kidding. It's not like that. Big Bambi doesn't go stalking anybody. What happens is, he gets rabies and he bloats all up —"

"Sara," Anita snorted, "you ready to go?"

Valducci put up his hands. "No — wait — wait. Honest, here's what *really* happens. Big Bambi grows old, see, and he becomes the world's first dirty old deer, and he goes around —"

"Sara!"

"No — wait — wait! He takes up karate, see, and every time he sees a hunter, he kicks the rifle out of his hands, and then — look — see" — he took a long french fry from Anita's bag and laid it across two soda cups — "every rifle he gets, he brings up his hoof and — *chakkah!*" Valducci chopped the french fry clean in half. "So," he said, looking all serious, "where you girls headin' for tonight?"

The girls couldn't help it — they were cracking up. They couldn't get their sodas up their straws without choking. And even Poff. He was rolling his eyes to the ceiling with this faint smirk on his lips — which for Poff is roaring, foot-stomping laughter.

Somehow, in the middle of all this, Valducci managed to herd me and Poff into the men's room.

"Okay," he said, "I got Anita. Who wants Sara?"

Poff grabbed my hand and shook it. "Congratulations." He headed for the door.

"Hey!" I called.

"Football. Eagles and Bears on TV. I'm goin' home."

So there I was, supposed to be out with Jennifer Wade, wanting to be out with Jennifer Wade, thinking and dreaming of Jennifer Wade — and stuck with Sara Bellamy.

Back at the booth, Valducci says, "You girls wanna go bowling?"

The girls discussed it with their eyes. Anita shrugged and took a last pull on her soda. "Okay."

We were halfway to Abbott Lanes when I said my first words of the night to Sara: "You bowl much?"

"Once in a while," she said. "You?"

"Not much," I said.

Actually, I'd never bowled in my whole life. I mean, I went to bowling alleys a few times, but not to *bowl*.

When we got a lane, Valducci took charge and wrote out the score sheet. He made teams; him and Anita, me and Sara. I didn't think much of it till I looked up. There, right above us, was this big screen with our score sheet projected onto it. There were our names, side by side, for all the world to see:

Sara   Greg

Suddenly I felt practically sick for the way I wanted things to be:

Jennifer   Greg

From then on, everything seemed to remind me of her. Other guys looking proud and cool with their pretty girlfriends. Even the weight of the bowling ball — it reminded me of pumping iron and sweating for her in my sweltering room all summer.

Megamouth's words kept haunting me: *"Lotsa cute boys over there in Conestoga."* Once, I half-imagined the pins were a bunch of cute Conestogans. I jerked the ball from the rack and slung it down the alley like it was a golf ball. It was my only strike of the night.

I left the group as often as I could. I went to the bathroom twice. I kept offering to go to the vending machines for food. Once, when I was heading back with popcorn, I almost had a heart attack. There, about ten lanes from ours, was Megamouth. She was bowling with her friend Sue Ann and Sue Ann's parents. In three seconds I was outside. I still can't remember what I did with the popcorn.

Nobody had to tell me what a rat I was being, vanishing on the others. But what else could I do? I was trapped in my own lie. I pulled out three hairs, one each for Valducci, Anita, and Sara. It was the least I could do.

I wanted to go home, but couldn't. Still too early to be coming home from a date. I prowled the streets for a couple hours. By the time I got home, I was roaring mad. I stormed into Megamouth's room. I'm not sure what I was planning to do (how do you mess up a dump?); I just remember kicking around stuff on the floor, and that's when I went flying. My head, just over my right eye, was the first thing to land. The next five minutes, I didn't have time to be hurt; I was too busy persuading my parents not to take me to the hospital and wiping blood out of my eye.

"What happened? What happened?" my father kept asking. I couldn't seem to make much sense of the question. I reached out and started moving some of the paper and clothes on the floor. I picked up a "Miss Piggy for President" T-shirt and there it was: a squished, half-eaten Twinkie.

I held up what was left of it for them to see. "I keep telling ya," I warned them, as a curtain of red fell over my right eye, "we're gonna get roaches."

Megin

IT WAS the first thing I saw when I went into the bathroom. It was dark brown and it was wrapped around the bristles — woven actually, in and out and around.

I heard my father leaving for work. I grabbed the brush and ran downstairs. "Daddy! Daddy! He did it again! That pig did it again!" I caught up to him halfway down the driveway. He turned and looked me up and down — mostly down — and gave me that smirky well-well-what-have-we-here look he uses when I'm doing something a little crazy. Like standing in the middle of the driveway early on a Saturday morning in my Wayne Gretzky nightshirt and bare feet with a toothbrush in my hand.

I jabbed the toothbrush at him. "Look!"

Still the smirky grin. "I'm looking, believe me."

"Stop it, Daddy. Here. The toothbrush."

"You trying to tell me I have bad breath?"

"Daddy, look!" I nearly mashed it into his eye. "*Look!*"

He recoiled, squinted. "Ah — yes. What *is* that?"

I stamped on the asphalt. "It's a hair! A big, brown, ugly, scummy *hair!*"

"Are you trying to tell me you have hair growing between your teeth? I thought puberty happened other places."

"DAD-DEEEE!"

That got to him. My father is a salesman, and salesmen think it's important to make a good impression, whether they're on the job or not. And how good an impression can you make if your kid is screaming her head off and wagging a toothbrush at you in her nightshirt in the driveway? I mean, would you buy a used washing machine from this man? So he dropped the smirk and started glancing nervously around the neighborhood. "Megin, you're going to get pneumonia."

"Daddy, the hair."

"Okay — what about the hair?"

"It's your proof. You're always saying I can't prove the stuff Greg does to me. Well, here it is."

"A hair?"

"Look at it. It's not Toddie's. It's not Mommy's."

"Could be mine."

"Daddy, do you want me to scream again?"

He took a deep breath. "Okay. So what now?"

Finally. I could smell justice. "So are you gonna punish him?"

"Oh, I don't know. For just a hair?"

"*Just* a hair? Daddy, there could be all kinds of rot on there. There's probably cooties on it right now."

"You could get cootiemouth."

That's when it happened: my lips smiled. Dirty traitors. I stood there helplessly as my dimples sunk deeper and deeper into my face. You could have stood ice-cream cones in them.

I tilted back, but my father's little finger was faster, poking into my left dimple. "Yeah — that's my Dimpus."

I ran down the driveway to the sidewalk. "Okay, I'm gonna scream."

My father came lurching after me, glancing around, holding his finger to his lips. "Shhhh-shhhh."

I backed into the street. "Gonna punish him?"

"*Megin!*" he whisper-called. He was frantic now.

"Are you?"

"Okay, okay."

"When?"

"Not now. I have to go to work."

"When?"

"Tomorrow."

"Tonight."

"Okay, tonight."

I was in the middle of the street now. My father was having an ulcer at the curb, terrified at what I might do next. Behind him I could see Mrs. Greeley peeping out her window.

"What are you going to do to him?" I said. I couldn't hear his answer. "Louder."

"I'll have to think about it."

A car turned the corner and started down our street. I wish I had a camera to record my father during the next ten seconds: he looked at the car, he looked at me, he looked at the sky, he turned around to walk back up the driveway and bumped into Mrs. Greeley's face at the window, he turned back, and as the car passed (slowly), he looked at it with an expression that I have never seen on his or any other human face before or since. He was still like that when I went past him and into the house.

I got a pair of tweezers and pulled the hair from my toothbrush. Then I waited for my mother to leave. This was her first day for her new project: ceramics class. Every Saturday morning.

When I heard the front door shut, I headed for the kitchen. I'm not allowed to use the stove by myself, but this was an emergency. I boiled my toothbrush in the egg poacher. I set the heat on high and pretty soon the bubbles were popping.

Meanwhile, I got my donuts. I have this job at Dunkin' Donuts. Lots of times after school and on weekends, I go there and fold boxes and stuff. Sometimes, when Jackie is on duty, I even get to help make the donuts. And best of all, I get paid in donuts. I had worked there the day before and had made my biggest haul ever: a dozen donuts. Assorted — not just all stale leftover glazed. (I love it when Jackie is on.) So, I got my donuts from under my bed and took them downstairs. That's when I noticed a peculiar smell. I rushed to the stove. The head of my toothbrush was an orange glop in the popping bubbles. All I pulled out was a stump.

I couldn't wait all day for my father to get home and start Grosso's punishment. I needed satisfaction — *now*. And I knew just how to get it. Torture. Donut torture.

Grosso loves donuts. All kinds. He never saw a donut he didn't love. And he was up in his room now, holding Toddie hostage by letting him watch cartoons on his TV set.

I couldn't help snickering to myself as I threw the orange stump away and set to work. First, I made two cups of tea, one for Toddie and one for me, and I used a tea bag for each of us. I put the cups and saucers real neat on the table, along with spoons and the sugar bowl and creamer. I even put a napkin under each spoon. And set out two plates.

Then, the donuts. I kept the french cruller in the box; I had other plans for that one. The rest of the donuts I laid in a row down the middle of the table — all eleven of them: one chocolate glazed, two blueberry-filled (my favorite), one cinnamon, one crème-filled, one raspberry-filled, one lemon-filled, one apple crumble, one peanut, and two plain-with-jimmies.

I was ready. I went upstairs, sat on the top step, and called: "Toddie." I could hear El Grosso telling him not to listen. "Shut up, Grosso! He's not your property!"

"He's in my room."

"You lured him in."

"It's not my fault if he wants to watch Road Runner."

"Toddie."

"Quiet. He's watching."

"Shut up and let him talk for himself!"

"Okay, Toddie," said Grosso, "do you want to go with Megin? Or do you want to stay here and watch Road Runner and Bugs Bunny and Yosemite Sam and Fat Albert?"

Out came Toddie's voice: "I'm stayin'!"

We'll see about that, I grinned to myself. "*Tah-dee*," I sang, "I have *doh-nuts.*" Absolute silence except for Coyote whistling off another cliff. I wiggled the bait. "Eleven donuts, Toddie. E-lev-en. All kinds."

"Don't listen, Toddie," I heard Grosso say. "She's lying."

His voice sounded a little parched. He wasn't really thinking about Toddie. He was thinking about the donuts. He was hooked.

"Eleven, Toddie. And we can have them all. Nobody else. Just us."

Silence.

"Five-and-a-half for you, five-and-a-half for me —"

Silence.

"All kinds, Toddie. Lemon-filled . . . raspberry-filled . . . peanut . . ."

Silence.

"Chocolate glazed . . . cinnamon . . ."

Silence.

"Apple crumble . . ."

Silence.

"Plain-with-jimmies. *Two* plain-with-jimmies. And *you* can have them *both*."

There he was, at the doorway, all eyes and grin and Winnie the Pooh pajamas. "Both?" he peeped.

"Both."

"Yippee!" He raced into my arms.

I lifted him up. "That's my boy. And guess what else I made for you?"

"What?"

"Tea."

"For me?"

"Yeah. Your very own."

"I'm not allowed."

"Yes you are. Mommy and Daddy are out this morning. I'm in charge."

"My own cup. Not just some of yours?"

"Your very own cup. It's on the table — now."

"Yippee!" He hugged me and smothered me with kisses.

"And I even forgot to tell you," I said as I carried him down the stairs, "we have a *crème-filled* too." I said "crème-filled" out loud to make sure El Grosso heard it. El

Grosso loves them all, but he would kill for a crème-filled.

When Toddie saw the table, he didn't say anything, but I think the look on his face was the same one my mother says I had when I first saw Christmas. Then a squeak came from Toddie and he made a beeline not for the donuts but for his teacup. He pulled his teabag up dripping from the steaming, amber-colored water.

"My teabag?"

"All yours."

Another squeak, and then he dipped the bag up and down about a hundred times into the tea.

Naturally Grosso showed up before long. And naturally he pretended he was just wandering in to get his breakfast. And naturally he just *had* to wander over to the table and pretend to look for the sugar bowl while he was really casing the donuts.

I could have stopped him, but I was enjoying watching him sweat. Usually when I bring home donuts my parents make me give him one, but since they weren't home — well, too bad, Grosso. I reached for the crème-filled and sort of passed it across his face. "Hmmm," I went. "Wonder if I should eat this now." (I could feel Grosso stiffen.) "Hope they didn't put *too* much crème in it. Hate it when they do that. Nah, I'll save it for last. Best for last." I put it back.

Suddenly the worst thing that could happen happened. I had to go to the bathroom. No point trying to wait it out. When my bladder says go, it means GO!

"Toddie," I said, grabbing his dipping hand (his tea was *black* by now), "now I only have a second, so listen. I'm going to the bathroom. If Greg tries to steal any of our donuts — any of them — while I'm gone, I want you to

40

yell. Understand?" GO — NOW! went my bladder. I ran.
"Remember — yell!"

Sure enough, as soon as I started to pee, Toddie yelled.
By the time I made it downstairs, the crème-filled was in
Grosso's hand, inches from his mouth.

"Put it down!" I told him.

"I'm allowed to have one."

"No you're not!"

"Mom and Dad said."

"They're not here!"

"It's a rule."

The donut was getting closer to his mouth.

"Put it down!"

Closer.

"Put it down!"

His mouth opened — the donut went partially in — I
reached, grabbed, squeezed, pulled — he bit. I never knew
so much crème could squirt out of one donut. Part of it
wound up on his face, and the rest hit the floor with a re-
volting plop.

He looked at the collapsed donut as if it were a dead pet.
I thought he was going to cry. A glop of crème was sitting
under his nose, blocking his nostrils, and as he started to
breathe harder and harder, the white glop sort of went in
and out of his nose. That's when it happened for the second
time that morning: my dimples caved in. I smiled, then
giggled, then laughed, then roared.

Meanwhile, Grosso started nodding and muttering,
"Okay, okay —" He dropped the dead donut in the sink —
"okay, okay" — squeezed the crème from his nose, and
wiped his face clean — "okay, okay." By now *I* was practically crying. My eyes were so teary I could hardly see him

as he reached for the table — "okay, okay" — then turned toward me — "okay, okay, o-KAY!" For an instant everything went black. He punched me! I thought. But if he punched me, why was Toddie laughing so hard, and why was the punch so soft, and why did it taste like blueberry?

I had been donuted.

As best I can remember, here's how the rest went: Grosso started to leave, but I stopped him with a raspberry-filled in the back of the head. Then he got an apple crumble in the left ear. Then I got a plain-with-jimmies down my Wayne Gretsky nightshirt. Then Toddie went completely bananas and started whipping donuts at both of us while he laughed hysterically. And then my mother was standing in the doorway. Silence, stillness, except for Toddie crying out, "Megin said I could have tea, Mommy! Megin said it!"

"I thought you had ceramics," I said, taking a handful of lemon filling from my hair.

"I was —," she started to speak, then looked down; one foot was smack in the middle of the original crème plop — "a week early."

My memory is a little fuzzy here, but I *think* I got a paper towel and knelt down and lifted up my mother's foot and cleaned off her shoe. And I *think* she just sort of turned and drifted away. And I *think* she left the house.

But I *know* exactly what I was thinking then: I'm never going to see my mother again.

Greg

OKAY, I'll come right out with it: I love Jennifer Wade.

It feels funny, saying the word *love* even to myself. I don't think I've ever used it before, at least not about me and another person. But it's the right word — love — yep, I'm sure.

I'm sure because I'm always thinking about her — when I'm eating toast, when I'm doing my algebra, when I'm taking a shower. And when I sleep, I dream about her.

And I'm sure because one night I awoke feeling clammy all over, my muscles ached, and I knew that even in the middle of a dreamless sleep my body was reaching for her. And so there, right there in the darkness, I held my pillow close and whispered, "I love you, Jennifer," and I kissed it.

The next night, in a dream, I heard her say, "I love you too."

That settled it. I put my weights back together and tore up the *Tradin' Times* ad. Next day I had study hall last period, so I left school early and pedaled my bike like mad for

Conestoga Junior High School. A little too mad, I guess. I zipped down a hill past some slow-moving cars and next thing I knew, I was being edged to a stop by a cop car.

The cop stayed in the car for a minute, doing things and speaking into his hand. Finally he came over, real slow, sort of sniffing and looking at his shoes and waving the cars on by. He smiled. "Waddaya say, chief?"

"Fine," I gulped. "Thanks."

"Nice bike there."

"Yeah? Thanks."

"New?"

"Nah, not really. Christmas."

"Ah, Christmas." He nodded. "I'm thinking about getting my kid one."

I was relieved. He just wanted to check out my bike for his kid.

"Sucker's fast, huh?" he said.

"Yeah, pretty. I guess. I don't know. Sort of."

"Bet you can crank it up real good, huh?"

"Yeah. Sometimes. Pretty good."

"Up to thirty maybe?"

"Better'n that."

He was impressed. "Yeah? Forty?"

"Forty-five," I said.

"No!"

"Yeah."

He whistled at the sky. "Ever break fifty?" he said, squinting into the sun.

"Nah. Someday, maybe."

"Like to, huh?"

"Mm — I don't know."

"Be quite an accomplishment."

"Yeah, I guess."

He looked directly down at me then and gave me the pleasantest smile I ever saw. "Congratulations."

He was holding out his hand. I took it. He shook it. "What for?" I said.

"You just did it."

"Did what?"

"You broke fifty."

"I did?"

"Fifty-one to be exact."

"Fifty-one? Me?"

"Yep, you." I was speechless. "That's a pretty fair hill you were going down there, chief."

"Was it?"

"Yeah, pretty fair. And those cars you were passing — notice anything about them?"

"Yeah, I did."

"What did you notice?"

"They were going too — uh — pretty slow."

He nodded. "That's right. Good. Now, uh, why do you think they were going so slow?"

"I was wondering that too," I said. "I figured it was a funeral, or maybe somebody real old at the head of the line."

He put his hand on my shoulder. A trace of pain came into his smile. "Sorry, chief. Wrong this time." He used his hand to turn me around till I was facing the direction I came from. "Look." There was the hill I had come down, and the slow-moving cars — and something else too. "What do you see?" he said.

"A sign."

"A flashing sign?"

"Yeah."

"Big?"

"Yeah."

"What does it say?"

"Fifteen."

"As in fifteen miles per hour?"

"Yeah."

"What else do you see?"

"A school."

"What kind of school?"

"Elementary."

"How do you know it's elementary?"

"The kids."

"What about them?"

"They're little."

"Yeah," he chuckled. "Little buggers, ain't they?"

"Yeah."

"Look at that one there — green jacket — running. He's downright tiny, huh?"

"Yeah."

"That bugger's so tiny, if you hit him he probably wouldn't even put a dent in your bike. Right?" My lip was quivering. "Right, chief?"

"Right."

I heard him sigh behind me. His hand gave my shoulder a squeeze and let go. "Fire or girl, chief?"

"Huh? What do you mean?"

"That much of a hurry, you must've been heading for a fire or a girl."

"Oh, uh, girl."

"Ah," he nodded. "Sure, girl. Name?"

"Uh, Jennifer."

"Jennifer. Nice name." Another squeeze on my shoulder. "Nice name."

Footsteps. He was walking away. But I couldn't turn. Couldn't face him. I heard his car start up, then pull away.

Needless to say, I didn't get to Conestoga that day. Next day, another last-period study-hall day, I tried again. A different route, still pedaling hard, but watching for school signs. I didn't get stopped by a cop, but I didn't see Jennifer, either. Too late. Place was deserted by the time I got there.

I had to leave earlier. I figured out a plan Next morning I'd tell my mother I was sick, couldn't go to school. Then around noon I'd have a miraculous recovery and tell her I was going to the library to study.

It worked. By twelve-thirty I was on the road. Then it rained. Hard. In a minute I was soaked. I didn't care. A little rain wasn't going to stop me. But a tidal wave did — the one that came shooting up from the back tire of a truck as it went through a puddle. It hit me in the face; I crashed into a trash can and wound up halfway across somebody's lawn.

Next day, I really *was* sick. I don't know if it was from pneumonia or discouragement, but I never made it out of bed. About four in the afternoon, I got a phone call. It was Sara Bellamy. I couldn't believe it. I had stayed away from her since stranding her at the bowling alley.

"Hi," I said.

"Hi. Didn't see you in school the last two days. You sick?"

"Yeah, a little, I guess."

"Getting better?"

"I'll live."

"That's good."

Silence on the line. Time to apologize. "Uh — sorry about, uh, taking off that time."

"Oh, that's okay."

"Something came up. I didn't have time —"

"Really, it's okay. Really." More silence. Then: "Greg?"

"Yeah?"

"You like fairs?"

"What do you mean?"

"Fairs. Games, booths, hot dogs."

"Yeah, I guess."

"Like to go to one? With me?"

"Gee, I don't know. What day will it be?"

"Saturday."

"Saturday, huh? Hmmmmm, Saturday . . . Saturday . . ."

"It's at Conestoga."

"What?"

"Conestoga Junior High. They have this fair every year. Remember Jennifer Wade? She went to our school last year?"

"Uh, I think so."

"She's a friend of mine and she goes to Conestoga now and she sent me tickets for some free games and stuff."

"Yeah?"

"Yeah. She's going to be working at a booth."

"Yeah? Which one?"

"The kissing booth."

Megin

IF ANYBODY saw me staggering under the pink-purple Dunkin' Donuts sign, they probably thought I was drunk. I flopped onto the nearest stool and slumped over the counter. Jackie's voice came like an angel's. "Hi there, Moxie."

"Hi."

"You look a little bushed."

"I'm dying."

"Shouldn't you be home for dinner?"

"Can't make it. I'm gonna die here if you don't mind. Just call the undertaker when I croak."

"That bad, huh? Lacrosse again?"

I tried to nod but I couldn't control it. My forehead hit something, a sugar container toppled from the counter. Jackie caught it.

"What's your number, Moxie?" she said.

"What number?"

"Phone."

I gave her my number. Somewhere in the distance I

heard a coin tinkle, then Jackie's voice: "Mrs. Tofer? .. she's here . . . Dunkin' Donuts . . . no, no problem . . . we'll feed her . . ."

Next thing I knew I was smelling something, not donuts. I opened my eyes: soup. "I hate soup."

A spoon waggled before my eyes. "Come on, take it. Now eat."

I took the spoon. "I hate soup."

"Moxie."

"I'm too tired to swallow anyway."

Jackie went away. When she came back she had half an old-fashioned in her hand. She broke it into pieces and dropped them into the soup. I started to eat.

"How many laps today?" Jackie said.

"Six."

"Wow! You must have really been a terror."

"They're all sissies."

"Coach too?"

"She's the sissiest. 'Tofer, take a lap. Tofer, take a lap.' "

"She likes you."

"She hates me."

"Why did she put you on the first team then?"

"She's afraid I'll beat her up if she doesn't."

Jackie laughed. "I believe it."

I sort of felt like laughing too, but my cheeks were too weak to sink a dimple. "They're all crybabies," I said.

"Maybe she thinks you ought to use your lacrosse stick on the ball instead of other players."

"Well, what's a stick for if you can't use it on some-body?" She just laughed. "Anyway," I said, "I never start it. If I had the strength to lift my leg up, I'd show you how many bruises I have."

"How's the soup?"

"Okay." It was great.

"Working tonight?"

"Too tired."

"I'll let you fill the blueberries."

Even Jackie had never let me do that. I looked at her. "You kidding?"

"Nope. I think you're ready."

Talk about temptation! I might have said okay, but just then I happened to look at the donut racks. The french crullers were gone!

Jackie saw the look on my face. She chuckled. "Hey, would I forget you?" She reached under the counter and brought up a fat, beautiful french cruller. "I saved it."

I sighed with relief. "Thanks."

"Say," she said, "how come you always want to take one of these with you? I thought blueberry-filled was your favorite."

"It is," I said, putting the cruller in my schoolbag.

"So?"

"So — my dog likes french crullers."

She cracked up. I was nearly out the door when I remembered, came back. "Hand," I commanded.

She gave me a grin and put out her left hand. The top half of the little finger was covered by a rubber thimble. I pulled it off and there it was: the most fantastic fingernail I had ever seen. It was long and tapered and perfect and deep red like the others, but that wasn't all. In the middle of it was a tiny, heart-shaped, sparkling stone — a fake diamond, I guess. You could always tell when she was filling donuts because that's when she put the rubber thimble over it. It was like a tradition for me to take a look at it each time I saw her.

"Wow!" I said. I touched it with my fingertip. "Man!" I

replaced the rubber thimble. "Gotta go." I left swooning from fatigue and the diamond fingernail.

The french cruller wasn't for me or a dog. It was for an old lady at Beechwood Manor, an old people's home nearby. I was passing the place one day soon after school started when I heard a voice. I thought it said, "Hey, pass me one." It didn't make any sense, and anyway, who would be talking to me around an old people's home? I kept on walking.

Next day, same thing: "Hey, pass me one." The voice was definitely coming from Beechwood Manor, and come to think of it, I *was* carrying my lacrosse stick over my shoulder. (We had to take them home each night the first week to "get the feel" of them. "Sleep with it," the coach told us. Not me, baby. I might sleep with a hockey stick, but a lacrosse stick — *never*.) Anyway, it was pretty creepy knowing that some senile old croaker was calling me from Beechwood Manor. I kept looking straight ahead.

Next day: "Hey, pass me one." I looked. A hand was waving from a second-story window. I couldn't see a face, but the voice said, "Over here. Come on."

Well, next thing I knew, I was up in her room. She was in a wheelchair and her name was — is — Emilie Bain. She told me she used to play lacrosse when she was a kid — her and the rest all boys. She said the Indians invented it. She took my stick and we played catch across her bed with a tangerine. She could catch and throw better with the stick than I could with my hands.

When she found out I work at Dunkin' Donuts, she rolled up real close to me and whispered, all excited, "Do you get them free?"

"Sure," I said.

"Any kind you want?"

"Sure."

She did a three-sixty in her wheelchair. "Can you get me ne?"

"Sure. What kind?"

Her face, especially her eyes, got all remembery and she idn't answer for a while. Then she said, "French cruller."

So that's how it is that I take a french cruller to Emilie very time I visit her. Actually, I have to smuggle it in, be- ause (as she whispered) they've put her on a diet and he's not allowed to eat anything good.

I don't know why I don't tell anybody about this. It vould just come out all snurdy, me and an old lady and a onut. If I ever do tell anyone, it will probably be Jackie.

Anyway, when I got to Emilie's room, I gave her the onut and flopped onto her bed. As usual, she offered me ome of her donut, but I didn't take any.

"You look like you just chased a jackrabbit," she said.

"Six laps," I groaned.

"Six? Only six? Fiddlefish."

"That means six extra, just for me. Besides the four verybody has to do."

"Still fiddlefish. That's only about two miles. I used to un that far just to reach the outhouse."

"Sure, Emilie, sure."

She was always saying crazy stuff like that, always tell- ng about the amazing feats of hers in the old days. Not hat I believed her, but she *was* sort of entertaining.

"Ever hear of Gresham, North Dakota?" she said.

"I hardly ever heard of North Dakota."

"Well, I used to live in Gresham."

"I thought you were from Long Island."

"I was, but we went to live in Gresham, North Dakota, for three years."

"So?"

"So that's where I caught a jackrabbit."

"So? What's the big deal about that?"

"With my bare hands. Ran it down on foot."

"Sure, Emilie, sure." I groaned and rolled over.

It sounded like her best story yet coming up. And it was. She said that when she went to North Dakota, she brought her lacrosse stick with her and pretty soon she had all the kids at the school she attended playing lacrosse — all the boy kids, that is. They made their own sticks. Then she taught the boys at a nearby Indian school. Then the boys at the two schools made up teams and decided to play each other, except neither of the teams wanted a girl — namely Emilie — playing for them.

So what did she do? She remembered reading how Indians sometimes used to catch animals just by running after them until the animal gave up. If she could catch a jackrabbit with her bare hands, she asked, would they let her play? The Indian boys said okay.

So that's what she did. There were plenty of jackrabbits around. The trick was to pick one out that didn't go diving right into a hole. After her seventh or eighth try, she found a real dummy that couldn't find a hole. Round and round, zig and zag they went across the prairie, all day — she was playing hooky — and just about the time school was out, the rabbit — she called it a "critter" — finally sort of curled up shivering and she just walked over and picked him up by the ears. She took the rabbit home and begged her mother to take her to a photographer. Then she let the rabbit go. When the Indian boys saw the picture, they let er join them, and she scored fifteen goals as they beat the other team 24 to 0.

It was fantastic enough just hearing a story like that, but to hear it coming from an old lady in a wheelchair — she's eighty-nine, she told me — well, if I weren't so tired, I probably would have burst out laughing. So I just came out with my little question that I ask when she gets too outlandish. "Emilie," I said, "what's it like to be old?"

Then I scrunched up and winced while she gave me the usual smack on my butt (not hard) and said, "How should I know? I'm not old."

Then I must have dozed off, because next thing I knew, Emilie was shaking me and telling me it's getting late and I better start heading home.

I don't even remember walking home and getting into bed. I didn't open my schoolbag until next morning at my locker. Besides the usual stuff, I found a plain, white envelope, which I couldn't remember putting there. I opened it and pulled out a picture, an old photograph, kind of faded and brown around the edges. It showed a girl about my age — pretty, short hair, wide-brim hat. She's giving the camera a grin so big and proud it almost stretches off her face, and in one hand she's holding up a jackrabbit by the ears.

Greg

I WAS EXCITED. I was nervous. I was happy. I was everything.

I pumped iron morning, afternoon, and night. I swear I could see my bi's growing before my eyes. My forearm vein looked like it was ready to pop out and slither away.

I Sassooned my hair every morning. I Close-upped my teeth every time I got near a sink. I Pro/Gained at every meal. Every morning: a Pro/Gain, raw-egg, wheat-germ shake. Raw vegetables. Raw fruit. Wherever I went: a potato skin in my pocket, a rubber ball in my hand.

One night Megamouth came home with donuts. My parents said she had to let me have my pick. One was crème-filled. I turned it down.

Meanwhile, *all* the while, I thought about the moment when I would step up to the kissing booth — and the kiss. What should it be like? Would my kiss impress her? Leave her wanting more? Turn her off? Would I just be the next pair of lips in line? Was she in touch with her spirit, our dream-life? Would our souls flow together through our lips? Would her eyes open, even before our lips parted, and see me, *really* see me, for the first time? And would she then, at that precise moment, *know?*

I went over the pros and cons of every type of kiss, from a tiny peck to a teeth-grinder. Once, I started to picture myself french-kissing her and I couldn't even finish the picture. I felt dirty, filthy, almost sick. I knuckled my head. No, scum, not her, not Jennifer Wade. You don't ever put your dirty paws or your grungy tongue on her. She stays pure and untouched until the day she marries you.

I started the countdown at 9:30 on Friday night. In twelve hours — 9:30, Saturday morning — Sara Bellamy and I would take the bus to Conestoga.

I tried going to sleep at 10:00. No use. I was too keyed up.

By 11:30 I was watching the news sign off on my TV. By 1:00 the late rock show was going off. I did sleep a little bit then, in between a gunshot here and a car chase there from the late-late movies.

By 5:30 A.M. I was wide awake, watching some guy explain how to tell when your flower is too big for your pot. I got up and did some lifting — seventy-five-pound deep-squats. There was a light tapping on my door, then my father's face. "Greg?"

"Yeah?"

"Know what time it is?"

"Yeah."

"You're lifting weights? Now?"

"Yeah."

He stared for a few more squats, then slowly closed the door.

At 6:00 I brushed my teeth — fast strokes along the gum line, like I read in *Reader's Digest* once. Brushed my tongue too. Then I flossed. Scooped out every nook and cranny. Used about two yards of string. I was spitting red, but it felt good, whipping my mouth into shape for the kiss. Then I brushed again to get rid of the flossed-out gunk. Then mouthwash. (Scope — minty, sweet; no mediciny breath for me) — gargle (green foaming mouth: mad teenager) — a final fast jolt of cold water — *ahhh!* In the history of mankind was there ever a more kissable mouth? Then I remembered; I hadn't eaten yet.

No problem. A little more mouthwork wouldn't hurt. Meanwhile, shower time. First I Sassooned my hair (1, shampoo; 2, conditioner; 3, rinse). Then, for washing, two soaps to choose from: Irish Spring and Camay. I went with the manly scent of Irish Spring. I tore the wrapper off a new bar. By the time I finished, the bar was about half gone. I really scraped out the crannies good, especially my belly button. Who knows what odor-causing bacteria were lurking in there? I probably dug out stuff that was in there since the day I was born.

I got out a new towel to dry myself. Then I blow-dried and combed my hair.

It was 7:00. The basics were over. Now for the details, the finishing touches. I clipped every nail on my body, all twenty of them. I dug out every speck of dirt from behind them, even the little toenails. I Q-tipped my ears. I Visined my eyes. I snipped all outlaw hairs on my head. I even thought about cutting my underarm hair a little shorter. I figured the longer they were, the more sweat they would collect and the smellier my pits would get. But then I thought about what Poff would think if he knew. Trash that idea.

Deodorant. I reached for my Sure aerosol. Gone! I stormed into Megamouth's room. I wanted to scream. How could I ever find it in that dump? Her shelves and closet were practically bare — everything was on the floor. I started kicking stuff aside: socks, Big Mac boxes, wet towels, papers, books, clothes, pretzels. Every time I moved something, I was afraid I'd uncover a nest of roaches. Finally I found my Sure, beneath the most gruesome lacrosse sock I ever saw and on top of three limp french fries. I gave her Wayne Gretzky poster a squirt in the face and got out.

At 7:30 A.M. I ate breakfast. My usual health shake, two boxes of raisins, and a potato skin.

Back upstairs, I redid my mouth. Then I figured I'd work on my vein, get it up so high that it would still be humping at the fair. That meant a hundred right-arm curls, minimum. After five or six curls, I suddenly had a problem: I was starting to sweat. I couldn't afford to sweat. A single sweat drop could bring on a million bacteria. By the time I reached the kissing booth, I'd smell like a garbage truck. On the other hand, I *had* to have my vein in top shape.

There was only one answer: a dumbbell in my right hand and my can of Sure in my left. After every third curl: squirt-squirt. The last twenty-five curls were pure murder, because by then I was getting a rash under my arm and it was itching, then burning, like mad. When I finally reached a hundred, I made a mental note to remember this day, in case twenty years from now I develop cancer of the armpit. I'll tell the doctors about the time I overdosed on deodorant. Maybe it will be too late to help me, but it might save others. Anyway, if it gets me twenty years with Jennifer Wade, it'll be worth it.

Then Toddie came in to watch his Saturday-morning cartoons. As soon as he sat down, he farted. Toddie can be amazing. Judging from the sound alone, you might have thought there was a horse in the room. Or an elephant.

Usually he says "Scooze me," but today he was all wrapped up in Daffy Duck. I shifted to the other end of the bed and didn't think much about it, until he farted again. Then again. Suddenly, as the invisible clouds drifted my way, I had a horrifying thought: It's seeping into my clothes! I could become a walking fart!

I got out of there fast. Then I remembered: my English Leather. I hadn't put it on, and it was back in my room. Luck was with me. It was on my dresser, just inside my door. I reached in and snatched it, and escaped just as Toddie cut another one.

Downstairs, I splashed my English Leather on everywhere, then left the house before anything else could happen. It was only 8:15, but that was okay. Sara's house was pretty far, and I could use a long walk in fresh air. I took a slow, roundabout way, and it was almost 9:00 when I saw Sara's house ahead. She was waiting on her porch. When she saw me, she jumped up, waved, hopped down from the porch, and came springily up the sidewalk. She was still ten feet away when she went, "Wow, you smell great!"

"Oh yeah?"

"Yeah. What is it?"

I shrugged. "I don't know. Some cheap stuff. Some spilled on me is what happened."

She chuckled and poked me. "Clumsy."

The bus stop was only two blocks away. She kept looking at me, smiling. "You're early," she said.

"Am I?"

"Yep."

"So are you."

Her smile went down a little but her eyes didn't. "Am I?"

When we finally got seated on the bus, Sara pulled something from her pocketbook. "Cert?"

She was staring at me. I stared at the pack. "Okay." I took one out.

"*Pas de quoi*," she said.

"Huh?"

"That's French. Means 'you're welcome.' 'Thank you' is *merci*."

"Oh. Thanks."

"*Pas de quoi*."

I didn't want to use the Cert yet, but she kept staring at me and somehow I knew she wouldn't stop until I put it in my mouth. So I did, and as soon as she turned away, I took it out and stored it in my pocket. I thought: In just a little while from now, a little drop of Retsyn will pass from my lips to Jennifer Wade's. I got a little dizzy just thinking about that.

From then on, the bus ride was mostly two things: me squeezing the rubber ball in my pocket, and Sara talking. Mostly about French stuff. I didn't hear much of what she said until I noticed how close we were getting to Conestoga. Then I started to get a little nervous, and then I thought I felt a sweat drop pop out under my arm. Stop thinking about it, I told myself. I turned to Sara and for the rest of the trip I nodded and raised my eyebrows and oh-yeahed at every word she said. I got the impression she was really into France.

"Maybe you oughta go over there someday," I suggested. "See the Eiffel Tower."

She laughed and poked me. "That's what I love about you, Greg, you're a great listener. I said a half hour ago I was hoping to do that."

The bus dropped us off near the school. Cars were parked all over, people heading for the gym door. As soon as we got inside, I knew I could forget my English Leather — it didn't have a chance with the smell of hot dogs, popcorn, and cotton candy.

Sara started pulling me. "Come on, let's go see Jennifer."

I held back. "Nah. Think I'll check out some other stuff first."

She waved one of her tickets in my face. "I can get you a free kiss from her."

I gave her a sneer. "Why would I want to kiss *her?*"

Her grin broke wide open, she whirled away.

There I was then, alone with an overwhelming feeling: *She's here. Somewhere. I'm in the same room with Jennifer Wade.* I gave my rubber ball ten good final squeezes and took off my jacket. My vein was bulging. I put the Cert in my mouth. I took a deep breath. I was ready.

I was wandering through the crowds, glancing around for the kissing booth, when I felt a tug on my shirt. Sara was behind me, grinning. Then a pout came over her face. "She's not here."

My heart stopped. "Who?"

"Jennifer."

"You sure?"

"There's another girl in the booth. She said Jennifer's sick. Phooey."

Then she said some other things, but I didn't pay much attention. I just sort of let her drag me around the place. I remember throwing some balls here, some darts there. I ate a tasteless something, drank a tasteless something else. Little kids reeled by in painted faces. Somebody went *thunk-splash* into a tub of water. A pony chewed straw.

Finally I said I had to get home. On the bus she kept it

up — staring at me, grinning at me, talk talk talk, cheery cheery cheery. I felt like stuffing my rubber ball down her throat.

I walked her to her porch. She wouldn't go right in. Ever since we had left the bus, she had stopped talking. And smiling. Now she was just looking. She leaned back against her front door. A new kind of grin, sort of shy, and a twinkle in her eye: "Uh, you know, you wouldn't need a ticket to kiss me." Suddenly that's what I was doing, kissing her. Her head banged against the door, my teeth clicked into hers. She gave a little yelp. Then I frenched her.

Megin

Romeo and Juliet Get Down and Boogie. That's what most of the kids wanted to call the show. But not Mr. MacWilliams. "I wrote it," he said, "and I'm naming it." So it's called *Romeo and Juliet — Now!*

It's supposed to be like the real *Romeo and Juliet* (by Shakespeare), only brought up to date. For instance, Romeo whams Whoppers at Burger King, and Juliet grills Big Mac meat at McDonald's, which is right next door. They arrange to take their breaks at the same time, and they meet in the shadows of a Dipsy Dumpster.

Romeo and Juliet have to meet in secret because their parents don't want them together. Romeo's parents are strict vegetarians. If they knew Romeo was working in a hamburger joint and fooling around with a meat-eater, they'd probably kill him. As for Juliet, her father's a butcher, so naturally he would never let his daughter near a vegetarian. I don't know what Shakespeare's show is like, but it *has* to be better than that. Anyway, that's about all I know, because soon after tryouts started, I got kicked off stage crew. Here's how it happened:

It was taco day in the lunchroom. Maybe that's why I got so mad. I love taco day, and I hate having it spoiled. Which is what Sue Ann did. How? By running off at the mouth again about the girl from California.

"Guess what?" she started.

Stupid me, I bit. "What?"

"Guess who's trying out for Juliet?"

"Miss Piggy."

"No," she said, not even cracking a smile at my little joke. "Zoe."

I swear she pronounced the name like she was praying in church. I honestly believe Sue Ann thinks Zoe Miranda is Mrs. God. "I'm impressed," I said.

"Well," she said, "isn't that goochy?"

"*Goochy?* Where'd you get that word? Never mind, I know."

And then we both said it: "Zoe."

"So what's *goochy* supposed to mean?" I asked her.

"It means, y'know, sensational. Really *something*. Y'know?"

"So why is it goochy that Zoe is trying out for Juliet?"

"Why? Man, Megin, don't you know—"

"Your taco, Sue Ann." If it's taco day, you can always tell when Sue Ann is getting hyper: she tips her taco more and more as she's eating it, till all the stuff starts falling out the other end.

She restuffed her taco. "Don't you know who Mr. Mac-Williams wrote the part *for?*"

"Miss Piggy."

"Maggie Wentzel."

Actually, I knew the answer. Everybody knows Maggie Wentzel wants to be an actress. "So?"

"So? So Mr. MacWilliams wrote the part *before* Zoe ever showed up from California. So *now* they *both* want to be Juliet. So *now* who's Mr. MacWilliams gonna *pick?*"

"Your Taco, Sue Ann. How should I know? That's his problem."

"Well, I'll tell you one thing—" Sue Ann's voice dropped to a whisper. "Maggie Wentzel hates her. *Hates* her. She wants to *kill* her."

"Great," I said. "At least there's one person who's not slobbering all over Zoe Miranda."

Sue Ann blinked. "What do you mean by that?"

"Groveling and sniveling."

"Megin—"

"Kissing her goochy butt."

"Megin, just because—"

"Taco."

"—because I talk about somebody doesn't mean I'm groveling and sniffing."

"Sniveling."

"You're just jealous, that's all."

"Yeah, right," I snickered, "I'm jealous. Because I can't wear silver sandals too."

"She's wearing shoes now."

"Right—silver ones. So what's next, silver boots? I'm really jealous of that. I wish I could worship Halley's comet too, and wear green toenail polish and anklets on both ankles and a ton of makeup. Yeah, I really wish it, no kidding."

Sue Ann's lower lip pouted out. "Yeah? I bet you wish you could wear a bra like her too."

"That so?"

"Yeah. You're jealous 'cause she's a *real* girl."

"Really? Since when did *you* start shopping in the lingerie department?"

"At least I *feel* like a girl."

"That so? What do you think I feel like?"

She burst out giggling. "Wayne Gretzky."

"Well here, feel this —" I reached across the table and mashed her nose in with my finger; then I shot my chair back and jumped up to leave. There was a jolt behind me, a screech, glass sliding, crashing, and suddenly my jeans were all warm and wet with taco stuff. Zoe Miranda was glaring at me through her green eye shadow. "You owe me a taco."

"You owe me a pair of jeans," I told her.

"You owe her a whole lunch," one of her grovelers butted in.

"Who asked you?" I shot back.

The California girl batted her green eyelids once. "You backed into me." She didn't raise her voice. She said it real slow, all calm and collected and silver shoes and bra sticking out and gold hoop earrings. "You backed into me," she repeated.

I couldn't think of what to say, so I just kept glaring at her, at her silly green eyelids. I noticed they weren't just green, they were *silvery* green.

"Whose fault *was* it?" piped up one of the other grovelers. She was asking Sue Ann.

We all turned. Sue Ann sat frozen at her place, her taco practically straight up and down, a little mountain of taco stuff growing under it. Her eyes were wide as windows; they kept shifting from me to Zoe. She didn't speak.

"You backed into me," came the calm, silvery voice.

The green eyelids were unblinking. *She's a real girl.*

She's a real girl. Then the words were coming out of my mouth: "You wanna fight?"

The green eyes grinned, the golden hoops hopped, the lipstick smirked. The silver girl from California turned and walked away. Her grovelers followed. They were laughing out loud.

I didn't speak to Sue Ann till next day, at stage crew. Tryouts were in the front part of the stage. We were in the back. Our job was to mix about a ton of shredded paper with flour in a couple big boxes. Later we would boil it in pots in the Home Ec kitchen to make papier-mâché, which would then be slapped onto a frame that the boys were working on. The whole thing was going to wind up as a five-foot-high Whopper.

Sue Ann didn't say anything. She couldn't even look at me. She just kept stirring her paper. I let her stew for a while, then I said, "Thanks a lot, Sue Ann."

"Huh?" she went, as if she didn't hear.

"You heard me."

"What do you mean?"

"You know what I mean." Her face was sinking deeper and deeper into her box. "You coulda stuck up for me, you know. You didn't have to go joining Zoe and her grovelers."

"I didn't join them."

I could barely hear her voice. "Well, you didn't exactly come racing to my rescue, did you? I thought I was supposed to be your friend."

"You are."

"Yeah, sure. You got a great way of showing it. The whole place was laughing."

"I wasn't."

"Well, I'll tell you one thing, it must make Zoe Miranda feel pretty powerful. Walking into this school and snapping her fingers and — zap — there goes my best friend. Excuse me, my *former* best friend."

"I *am* your best friend."

"Traitor."

"No!"

She was starting to cry. It's an old trick of Sue Ann's, whenever she wants sympathy. Trouble is, I always fall for it. So in another minute or two, it was like nothing had happened. We were laughing and throwing shredded paper and making fun of the auditioners. We could hear them but we couldn't see them, because between us and them were all kinds of scenery junk, including the McDonald's golden arches. They were the first thing the stage crew made. They were huge.

At first the Romeos were trying out. Each one had to do a speech and sing a song, "Whopper Woo." Every couple minutes, even in the middle of the song, we could hear Mr. MacWilliams's booming voice: "Val-dooo-cci!"

I don't know why Mr. MacWilliams did it, but he put El Grosso's idiot friend Valducci in charge of the lighting. That's why the stage lights were always changing colors, like we were in a disco or arcade. And that's why the spotlight was never where it was supposed to be, but roaming all over the place: on the auditioners in the wings, the walls, the ceiling, the back of Mr. MacWilliams's head. Sometimes a sliver of spotlight would reach all the way back to us. "Val-dooo-cci! . . . Val-dooo-cci!"

The Juliets came after the Romeos. Their song was "Squeeze Me, Please Me, Cheese Me." Maggie Wentzel did it first. She was great. I would have given her the part right there. Then it was Zoe's turn. Sue Ann and I stopped mixing paper to listen.

"I don't think she's so hot," I said. Sue Ann just shrugged. I jabbed her. "She's really rotten, isn't she?"

She shrugged again. "Sort of."

I laughed. "Come on, Sue Ann, tell the truth. I won't get mad."

She grinned. "I think she's great."

"She *stinks.*" I laughed and kicked over her box.

Suddenly her face broke out in horror. She pointed to the floor and squealed: "Look out!" Something was heading away from the kicked-over box and straight for me. A roach! A BIG roach! I jumped up and backed away. That's when I tripped over something, and next thing I knew I was stumbling backward. I couldn't stop. Behind me, Zoe was into the long, final high note of the song. Then I banged into something else and fell. World War III. Crashes all around. But the high note never stopped. I looked up in time to see a big scenery panel fall forward, and there was the bright-lit stage front, with Zoe Miranda singing the high note out toward Mr. MacWilliams in the auditorium, her arms high in the air, her fingers spread out. Down came the golden arches — slowly, like they didn't really want to — and as they came down, Mr. MacWilliams came up, and as they toppled down over Zoe Miranda like a giant halo, she never flinched, never stopped singing. The crash of the golden arches and the end of the note came at the same time.

Dead silence. Zoe Miranda, arms still up, was turning slowly toward me. Then everything went white: the spotlight was on me. And out of the blinding light came Mr. MacWilliams's booming voice: "Out! *Tofer! OUT!*"

70

It took me about three seconds to scramble around for my book bag and get out of there. The spotlight followed me all the way. In fact, even as I was walking home, I could have sworn it was still on me.

Sue Ann slept over that night, along with her monkey, of course. We were all serious at first, her apologizing for screaming and getting me in trouble, me telling her to forget it. Then she started grinning at me. "Megin?" she said.

"Huh?"

"Can I tell you something?"

"Speak."

"You wouldn't *believe* how funny it looked. You stumbling backward and all."

"I couldn't stop."

"I know."

"I was trying to stop and not fall on my butt at the same time."

"I know, I know!"

"I crashed!"

"Ka-boom!"

"And the scenery! Everything!"

"Ka-boombah!"

We howled.

It was while we were howling that I reached into my book bag and pulled out a half-eaten Milky Way. Something else came out too: a roach. Probably *the* roach. It plopped onto some paper — you could *hear* it — and disappeared. I blinked through my laughter tears. "Omagod."

Sue Ann saw it too. "Eeeek!" She jumped onto a chair. "Megin! Kill it!"

"Kill it? I gotta find it first." I started kicking stuff aside. "Come on."

"I'm not coming down there! I'm scared to death of roaches!"

"I don't exactly love them either, bozo, but we gotta get it or I'm the one that'll get killed. Grosso's always saying we're gonna get roaches because of me."

She still wouldn't come down, so I gave her my hockey stick. She started swishing through the floor stuff. "If you see it, mash it," I told her — but at the same time, an idea hit me. "No, don't mash it." I ran to the bathroom and brought back a paper cup.

"What's that for?" she squealed.

"Never mind. Just find the roach. And *don't* mash it."

Well, for the next ten minutes it was "Megin, there! . . . Megin, there!" and each time I looked "there," the roach was gone. But finally I got it — I gave Sue Ann's monkey a shake and out it fell. I pounced like Gretzky on a loose puck — down came the paper cup. The roach was trapped.

One by one I pulled the papers and stuff out from under, till there was nothing but an old postcard beneath the roach. I lifted the postcard, keeping the cup clamped to it, and carried the roach out of my room, down the hallway, to El Grosso's room. He was inside. The door was shut. I crouched. I pressed my little surprise to the threshold. I tilted the postcard, lifted the cup. The roach ran under the door.

Greg

I DIDN'T KNOCK on my parents' door, I just barged in. They were still asleep. I stood at the foot of the bed.

"I told you it would happen." Nobody moved. Louder: "I told you it would happen." My mother's head came out from under the covers, raised, tilted toward my father's head, lowered, disappeared. *Louder:* "I told you it would happen." This time when my mother's head came out, she squinted down the covers to me. She blinked but didn't speak. "I told you it would happen."

She said something; I think it was "What?"

"Roaches."

"Huh?"

"Roaches."

She looked at the clock, looked at me, blinked. "Huh?"

"Roaches."

She blinked some more. Her head slowly turned away and lowered. She must have given my father a good jab under the covers, because he suddenly jerked awake. He

73

looked at her, but by this time her head had disappeared again. Then he noticed me. "Greg?"

"Roaches."

"Isn't it early?" He looked at the clock. "Saturday morning?"

"Roaches."

He looked up, scanned the ceiling. "Roaches?"

"Yeah. She finally did it."

"Who?"

"Your daughter."

"Did what?"

"Roaches."

"Roaches." His eyes shifted around. "Where?"

"My room."

"You saw them?"

"It. But where there's one, there's more. Maybe hundreds."

"Weren't you sleeping?"

"Yeah. I just opened my eyes for a second. There it was."

"Maybe you were dreaming. A nightmare."

"I was awake. It was real. On the windowsill. I saw something moving. I got up and looked. That's what it was."

"Maybe it was a water bug. They look like roaches."

"Water bugs are slow. Roaches are fast. This was fast."

"Did you get it?"

"No. Couldn't find anything to hit it with in time."

He closed his eyes, yawned. "What's a roach doing up this early?"

"It's not funny."

"Sorry."

"I told you this would happen. You wouldn't listen."

His head was going back down. "I guess not."

"You're calling an exterminator, aren't you?"

"Too early."

"Maybe they have twenty-four-hour emergency service."

"That's tow trucks."

"Maybe exterminators too. It's a health hazard."

"One roach? Emergency?"

His head was gone now. I was talking to a blanket. "It's an emergency for me."

"Okay, we'll see."

"Well, I'm not sleeping in that room till we get an exterminator." I left.

I was back in a minute, up at the head of the bed this time, holding a pizza crust I had snatched off Megamouth's floor. "Here — look."

An eye came out. "What's that?"

"Pizza."

"No thank you."

I jabbed it in his face. "Dad — I got this off her floor. This is why we got roaches now. Next'll be diseases. They're having the World's Fair for Bacteria in there."

"I'll talk to her."

"*Talk* to her? That doesn't do any good."

"I'll see that she cleans her room."

"What good's that do? You're always telling her to clean her room. She doesn't. It stays garbage in there."

"I'll make sure this time."

"How?"

"I'll take her garbage license away."

I stormed out. From the doorway of Megamouth's room, I winged the pizza crust at the bed. There was a bleat, but the head that popped up and turned to face me wasn't

Megamouth's — it was her friend Sue Ann's. I hardly got the word "Sorry" out before Megamouth was standing on the bed in her grungy Gretzky nightshirt with her fists clenched. "Waddaya think you're doing?" she squawked. She turned to Sue Ann. "What'd he do to you?"

Sue Ann was holding her ear and gawking at me like I was a great white shark. "I don't know," she whimpered. "Something hit me."

"Don't worry," I said, "it wasn't meant for her, it was meant for you."

Megamouth looked around, saw the crust, picked it up, and fired it at me. I ducked. "Get outta here!" she yelled.

"I'll get outta here when that roach gets outta my room."

"That's *your* problem!" She threw a pinecone at me. While I was coming out of my duck from that, something else headed my way: brown, furry, legs. I caught it in the face. My first thought was, My God, she even has a dead dog in here! Then Sue Ann was going, "Megin — not my monkey!"

I whipped the monkey back at her. It's hard to aim a monkey. It missed her by five feet and knocked off the only thing left on her dresser, some stupid picture of some kid holding a rabbit. She stared at the picture for a second; next thing I knew she was heading for my throat. But then my father was there, pulling us apart, stuffing her back into her room, shutting her door, herding me away.

Later, in the kitchen, my mother was pouring my father's coffee and saying, "I don't see how I can go to ceramics today. This time it won't be donuts. This time they'll kill each other."

"That's a trifle overreacting," my father said.

"Tell that to my headache. And I was supposed to use the kiln today."

"Sibling rivalry, honey."

"Sibling homicide."

I was at the refrigerator. I heard a fart. "Hey, Toddie me boy!" my father cackled. "Listen, I want you to go up to Greg's room and do that again. Then shut the door real quick. Any life forms in there ought to be dead within five minutes."

"Thanks," I said. I grabbed a handful of grapes and left. "Don't worry about us fighting if you go. I won't be here."

I spent most of the day at the library, doing research.

At dinner that night, my father plunked down a can of bug spray.

"That's no good," I sneered. "Roaches became immune to that stuff a long time ago."

"How's that?" he said. "Did they all get vaccinated?"

Megamouth snickered.

That's how it went, him giving his supposedly clever comments to my library notes: that roaches have been around for over 300 million years ("Hey, that's a mighty old roach you got up there"); that a female roach lays fifty eggs at one time ("Whew! That's a lot of diapers to change!"); that they contaminate everything they touch ("Like teenagers, huh?"); that they even eat the glue off book bindings ("Don't bookworms do that?").

Finally I crumpled up my notes and got up to leave the table. "You're not going to call an exterminator, are you?"

My father held out the can of bug spray. "Let's just try this first. I hate to spend twenty to thirty dollars on one bug."

"It won't work." I walked away.

He called. "Greg?"

"What?"

"Just one question. You said they hang around where it's all dirty and wet and garbage?"

"Yeah, so?"

"So how come the roach went to your room instead of Megin's?"

"Yeah, how come?" piped Megamouth.

"Because it didn't *go* to my room," I said. "She *put* it there."

Megamouth shrieked. "Liar!"

"How do you know?" said my father.

"I know."

"But *how* do you know?"

I grabbed my jacket and slammed the door on the way out.

They thought I was kidding. I wasn't. I slept on the living-room sofa that night. I kept thinking of the roach making itself at home in my room, getting fat on the bindings of my books. Sometimes I felt really bitter and was ready to charge upstairs and retake my room, but thinking about the roach crawling over me in my sleep — maybe across my face — was enough to keep me on the sofa.

I also kept wondering how my father could not believe Megamouth was behind all this. (He hadn't even made her clean up her room.) Didn't he see that the fact that the roach was in my room *proved* that she planted it there? Because what roach, if it had a free choice of rooms, would pick mine over Megamouth's? What were my book bindings compared to her garbage? That would be against all nature.

Well, during the next morning the picture changed a little. I was in Sunday school, and we were talking about the plagues in Egypt, when the land was overrun by locusts and frogs and stuff. The plagues were God's punishment on Egypt, the teacher said. That's when it hit me: maybe the roach *was* planted in my room, but *not* by Megamouth.

That started me wondering what I'd done lately worth getting a plague-type punishment for. It didn't take me long to think of something. In fact, it had been in the back of my mind all week: the way I'd treated — the way I'd *used* — Sara Bellamy. Just because I wasn't crazy about her didn't mean I had a right to take advantage of her, just so I could get to Jennifer Wade. I was a rat.

I made a vow to be honest with Sara. No more leading her on. I would ignore her, make it plain that she ought to forget about me, clear my conscience.

Monday morning — I slept on the sofa again Sunday night — that's what I did. I saw her in Algebra, in the hallways twice, and at lunch. Each time, I looked the other way, waved at somebody else, pretended to be talking to others. I could see the shock on her face. Pain too. It was hard. Sara Bellamy is an okay girl, even if she's not my type. I really had to force myself to remember that I was doing this for her sake. I was thankful that she didn't try to talk to me, that she wasn't making it harder than it already was. Class girl, Sara.

By afternoon I was feeling a little better, a little lighter. Like in the conscience, maybe? And for an instant I had the strangest feeling that half a mile away a certain cockroach was leaving my room.

Then, as I was coming out of History, I felt a tap on my shoulder. It was Sara. Usually I wouldn't see her there. She must have come looking for me.

"Hi," she said. Her lips were smiling, but her eyes were wider than usual. "*Bonjour.*"

"Oh, hi," I said.

"Preoccupied today?"

"Who, me?"

"Yeah, you," she mocked.

I shrugged. "I don't think so."

"Sick?"

"Nope."

"Worried?"

"Never."

"Enjoying this third degree?"

I laughed. "Sure."

Her smile changed. "Something wrong?"

"What could be wrong?"

"I don't know."

"Well," I chuckled, "I don't know either."

"You're not mad?"

Her eyes were burning into mine. I laughed. "Shoot, no. What at?"

"Me, maybe?"

"Heck no!" I nudged her.

We both laughed. We walked a ways, laughing. Then she said, "Well, glad that's settled."

"Yep."

"Yep. Now I can invite you to my party." She saw the shock on my face. She laughed. "Freaky fifteen. You're the first to hear about it. Saturday night. Coming?"

I wish I could say I said "Sure" instantly, the moment she asked me, laughing-eyed. But I didn't. First a thought came to me: *She'll probably invite her friend Jennifer Wade too.* And only then, *then,* did I say, "Sure."

And half a mile away a certain cockroach turned around.

Megin

DADDY, it's not *my* fault."

"I didn't say it was."

"So why are you punishing *me?*"

"I'm not punishing you."

"You're making me clean my room."

"That's punishment?"

"What do you know? You never have to clean a room. Mommy cleans your room for you."

"Well, when you get married you can have your husband clean your room. For now, it's up to you."

There was more to it than he was saying, something he wasn't telling me. "Daddy, the roach is in *his* room. Not mine."

"I know, but it's not that simple."

"You think I put the roach in his room, don't you? You believe him."

"I didn't say that."

"You never believe me. You're against me."

He took a deep breath. He put his hand on my knee and

patted me. I slapped it away. "Dimpus — honey — I'm not against anybody. It's just that for three nights now Gregory has been sleeping in the living room."

"So?"

"So, it bothers me. It's not right. He has a room. He should be sleeping in it."

"So, make him."

"It's not that simple. He's really terrified of roaches."

"So get an exterminator."

"It's not that simple either."

The way he half-grinned, the way he looked at me, I could tell I was close to what he was holding back. "Why isn't it that simple?" I said.

"Well, because Greg feels an exterminator —"

"Oh, *Greg* feels."

"— an exterminator isn't enough. It's okay to have an exterminator, but first we ought to have all the other rooms in the area as clean as possible."

"Oh, great. So *he's* giving the orders now, huh? *He* tells *you* to tell *me* to clean my room. What are you, his slave? I thought you were the father around here."

"Honey," he whined, "why are you making such a big deal out of it anyway? I'm not asking you to commit suicide. All I'm asking is for you to clean your room."

"That's not the point."

"Okay, what is the point?"

"The point is, I'm being persecuted for something I didn't do. I'm being framed."

He laughed. "In the first place, you're not being persecuted. In the second place — look, Dimpus — just do it for me, okay? A favor for your old dad. Okay?"

He was staring at me, wanting me to smile back at him

and say, "Okay, Daddy." He'd have to wait about a million years. "It's not fair," I told him.

"Life's not fair."

"It stinks."

"Life stinks."

So, strictly as a favor, I cleaned my room. When I finished I went to him. "Okay, it's done."

He looked like he didn't know what I was talking about. "What's done?"

"Waddaya think? My room. You told me to clean it."

He looked at the clock. "That was five minutes ago. You're *done?*"

"Come on and see."

He came, he saw, and he laughed. I asked him what he was laughing at. He tweaked my cheek. "You're getting to be quite the little comedian, Dimpus. For a minute there, I thought you were serious." He went away laughing.

"What're you gonna do?" I called. "Have a big laugh with Grosso?" I reached my foot under my bed and kicked out the stuff I had pushed there.

That night, I finished my dinner in two minutes and got up to leave. I told them I was going to Dunkin' Donuts.

"I don't think so," my father said.

"What?" I screeched. "Why not?"

"Your room."

"What about it?"

"You know what about it."

"I *did* clean it. I showed you."

"You might have done something to it, but I don't think the word is *clean.*"

I turned to my mother. "Mom, can I go?"

Her fork cut a piece of broccoli in half. "You heard your father."

"But I *have* to go to Dunkin' Donuts. I *have* to." (I hadn't taken a french cruller to Emilie in a week.)

"Fine," my father said. "Just clean your room and you can go."

"So I can't go, huh?"

"Dimpus, come on now, be a good girl."

My eyes felt hot. "So. I can't go." I grabbed a buttermilk biscuit. "I can't go to Dunkin' Donuts because *he*" — I pointed at Grosso — "says I have to clean my room. *He* says." I fired the biscuit at his head and stomped out of the room and up the stairs. Behind me I could hear glass smashing and my mother crying out and Toddie laughing and chairs knocking and my father holding Grosso back.

No one bothered me that night. Just me and Emilie's picture on my dresser. How lucky she was! What a kidhood! Out there in North Dakota, the prairie — no roaches, no brothers, no problems. I kept looking at the huge smile on her face, her eyes staring right at me, like she was saying, "Come on, Megin, come on out here. Let's chase some critters, you and me!" Emilie never let people get the best of her. She never would have cleaned her room just because some brother was afraid of a bug. Not Emilie.

When I got home from lacrosse practice next day, Toddie kept giving me that silly smirk. Pretty soon I found out why. Inside my room was a broom and a plastic trash bag. Each had a cardboard sign in blue crayon letters. The signs said BROOM and TRASH BAG. I yelled to the whole house from my doorway: "*I was gonna clean my room tonight but I ain't gonna now!*" I threw out the broom and bag and slammed the door.

They only called me once to come to dinner. They knew better than to try to force me. Toddie came up with a tray. He knocked on the door and left it outside. I could hear him running back downstairs.

I think I heard Grosso and my father arguing later that night. Grosso slept on the sofa again.

Next night I ate dinner with them. Nobody said anything. There were no biscuits on the table. When I finished and got up, my father said, "Tonight, Megin. Do it now."

"I have homework," I said.

"It can wait."

"You want me to flunk?"

"Clean your room. Now."

He wasn't smiling.

I don't know how long I was in my room, sitting on the bed. The door opened. It was my mother, of all people. "Can I come in?"

"Nobody's stopping you."

As she came toward me, something crunched under her foot. She winced but kept coming. She sat down on the bed. She folded her hands in her lap and sort of sightsaw around the room, like it was a strange place she was visiting for the first time, which was practically the case. She spotted Emilie's picture. "Say, who's that?"

"A friend of mine."

"Oh. Gee, looks like an old picture."

"So?"

"Can I pick it up?"

"It's a free country."

She picked it up like it was a bubble. She seemed fascinated. "It's a girl, isn't it?"

"Wha'd you think it was?"

"I guess I thought it was a boy at first."

That bothered me. "Why?"

"I don't know. Short hair, I guess. The hat." She shook her head. "What a picture. Is it real?"

"No, it's fake. It's gonna disappear any minute."

"I mean was it staged? Is she wearing a costume? Is that a real rabbit?"

" 'Course it's a real rabbit," I sneered. "A jackrabbit."

She looked at me, amazed. "Really?"

"She caught it with her bare hands. Running. In North Dakota."

She kept staring at it, still amazed. She put it back but didn't take her eyes off it. "I, uh, thought maybe you could use some help," she said at last.

"What with?"

"Your room. Cleaning it."

This wasn't making any sense. "Why do you want to do that?"

With the toe of her shoe she lifted a sweat sock and dangled it off the floor. "Oh, I don't know. I just thought maybe you were having a hard time." She looked at me. Right at me. I couldn't remember the last time my mother had looked at me that way. "You could use a little help, couldn't you?"

All of sudden, crazy, I was crying. And blurting; "I tried — a couple times — I started — but I couldn't — I couldn't —"

She put her hand on my knee. "You couldn't finish."

"No."

"You wanted to."

"Yes."

"But you couldn't."

"No."

"You just . . . *couldn't*."

"No!"

I bawled even harder. She let me go on for a while, stroking my knee. Then she said, "Know what?"

"What?"

"You have cleanophobia."

"What's that?"

"Fear of cleaning your room."

Jeez, now I was laughing, even though I was still crying. What was going on? Why was she doing this to me?

"Tellya something," she whispered. "I used to have cleanophobia too."

"Yeah?"

"Yeah. Hated to clean my room. Maybe not really hated it — just couldn't. Didn't know how. I had a mental block, I guess."

"That's probably what I have."

"My poor mother, she gave up telling me to clean it. She just kept the door to my room shut all the time."

"That's what you do."

She nodded and grinned.

"So," I said, "can I go to Dunkin' Donuts now?"

She laughed. "Why is it so important to go to Dunkin' Donuts?"

"Because I have to get a french cruller."

"I didn't know you were so crazy about them."

"I'm not." I nodded at the picture. "It's for her."

"Her?"

"Yeah. Her name's Emilie." And then I told her about me and Emilie and the jackrabbit story and lacrosse and the Indian boys and all.

When I was done telling, she got up, clapped her hands

and said, "Okay, first we'll clean the room — together — and then we'll go to Dunkin' Donuts, and then we'll go see Emilie."

All I know is, I worked my butt off and did everything she told me and after a while she said, "That's it. It's clean."

I looked. "It is?"

She laughed. "Try to remember now — *this* is what a clean room looks like."

Off to Dunkin' Donuts. Jackie snuck us two french crullers. She also gave us a bag of day-old honey-dipped. Before we left I made her show my mother her diamond fingernail. She didn't want to, but she did. My mother was very impressed.

Emilie was her usual outrageous self. She snatched the crullers out of my hand, whipped the door shut, and gobbled them down right then and there. Only after that did she seem to notice my mother. And what's the first thing my mother said to her? "Did you really catch that rabbit with your bare hands?" I almost kicked her in the shins.

But Emilie was nice. "Oh sure. Bare feet too. After the first hour or so chasing the critter, I took off my shoes. Boots actually. Then afterwards I went looking for them, but I couldn't find them." She chuckled. "Probably some gopher took them."

"You never told me that part," I said.

"Maybe not. It's hard to remember all the parts at once."

"Still," said my mother, "it's amazing."

Emilie smacked her hand on a wheel. "You're right. Amazing. That's what I keep telling Megin. She didn't believe me at first."

"I did so," I told her.

She grinned at me. "Anyway, I never said I was faster

than the critter. I just wanted to catch him more than he wanted to get away from me, I guess."

I told Emilie about my room and the whole hassle and my disease. I asked her if she'd ever had cleanophobia.

"Honey," she said, "I had it so bad I almost died of it!"

The three of us almost died laughing.

"You're lucky," I told her. "You don't have brothers."

"Who says I don't?" she snapped.

I was astounded. "You do? You never said anything."

"Well," she said, "maybe that's because he's not worth talking about. He was just a baby out in Dakota, so he wasn't much good to me. And now all he does is tell me to stay on my diet. No french crullers from him."

"He visits you?" I said.

"Sure. All the time. You'll probably bump into him one of these days."

Emilie was glancing around the room, looking antsy. I knew what was on her mind. I nodded toward the doorway. "Emilie, shall we show her?"

Emilie's eyes twinkled from my mother to me. "Check the hallway," she said.

I checked. "It's clear."

"Let's roll."

I told my mother to stay and watch from the doorway. I pushed Emilie out of the room and down to the far end of the hallway. I swung her around. The whole long hallway was before us.

"Flaps down?" I called.

"Flaps down."

"Brake light off?"

"Brake light off."

"Parachute?"

" 'Chute."

"Ready for takeoff?"

"Roger."

"Geronimo!"

A good heave and off we went. I pushed faster and faster as we passed the first five or six doors, then I climbed aboard the back and we went sailing and waving past my mother's horrified face. About three doors from the end, I hopped off and brought us to a perfect stop.

Wheeling back to the room, I called out before my mother had a chance to holler at me: "It was *her* idea! Right, Emilie?"

"Right," said Emilie.

"We do it all the time, right, Emilie?"

"Right."

"And guess what, Mom? Guess what we're gonna do next?" My mother just kept gaping at us. "I'm gonna teach Emilie to play ice hockey. Soon as Homestead Lake freezes over. Right, Emilie?"

"Right."

When we got back home, the sheet, blanket, and pillow were gone from the living room. On my bedroom door there was a blue ribbon and a sign that said:

1st PRIZE
WORLD'S CLEANEST
ROOM

Greg

THE EXTERMINATOR was on his way out when I came home from school on Friday. I asked him if he'd seen the roach. He said no, but not to worry. He patted his silver tank. "No bug could ever live through that." Maybe not, but I'd still have felt a lot better if I could've seen the corpse.

So, since the roach was dead (supposedly) and Megamouth's room was clean (supposedly), and since I was sleeping in my room again and everybody was happy (supposedly), and since my father's one free Saturday a month was coming up tomorrow, he decided we should all go for a drive in the country.

He was at his most gruesome, cheerful worst the next morning. He let Toddie have whatever he wanted for breakfast, which turned out to be tea and licorice. He kept tickling Megamouth to make her laugh and show her dimples. And he kept giving me little punches in the arm and asking me serious questions about weightlifting and health food.

Most of this stuff slid off me, since my mind was on other things. Such as Sara's birthday party that night and a certain person named Jennifer Wade, who, just as I figured, was also invited. Only one thing I wanted to know from my father: What time would we be home? Six o'clock, he said. No problem. The party wouldn't start till eight.

I knew my father was really off his rocker about this happy-little-family business when I saw his seating arrangements for the ride in the country: my mother up front with him, the three kids in the back. That might not sound like a big deal, but for us it was front-page news. Usually one kid sits in front and my mother sits in the back, in the middle. That way, no matter how you look at it, no two kids are right next to each other. It's how my mother survives long car rides. Short ones too.

"No, Frank," she kept saying, trying to be pleasant but also trying to climb into the back seat. "I think it's enough that we're all in the same car." But my father wouldn't let her. Not that he physically stopped her, but he was just so nice and smiley and peachy about the happy little Tofers that she finally stopped arguing and dumped herself into the front seat.

We hadn't even reached the end of the driveway before the first fight started. Toddie was in the middle of the back seat, but of course he wanted a window. So, nice guy that I am, I put him on my lap. Sure enough, Megamouth started screaming, "Mom! He's taking Toddie!"

"What do you mean *taking* him?" my mother said. Every once in a while, when my mother decides to deal with us, she tries using logic.

"Just what I said," Megamouth ranted. "He's taking him."

"You mean," said my mother, "like *stealing?*"

"That's right. He's stealing him."

"Well, do you mind me asking, how can he steal his own brother?"

Megamouth stomped her foot. "You know what I mean. He doesn't have a right to pull Toddie out of his seat."

"Toddie," my mother called, not turning around, "did Greg pull you out of your seat?"

"Say no," I whispered to Toddie.

"No," answered Toddie.

"Mom! He's telling Toddie what to say! He's whispering to him!"

"Is Greg whispering to you, Toddie?"

"No," I whispered to Toddie.

"No," said Toddie.

Megamouth stomped both feet. Spit flecks were shooting from her mouth. "Mom! Jeez — turn around — look! He's even laughing at you! Look!"

It was true. I was grinning like a champ, because I knew my mother would never turn around. Which she didn't. All she did was tilt her head toward my father and say, "There's your happy little family, dear."

Megamouth didn't know what to do next. The parts of her face were twitching and jerking in fifty different directions. Her skin was changing colors. I thought she was going to disintegrate right there in the back seat. She snarled at Toddie and sort of hissed through clenched teeth, "Don't you ever come over on this side." And then she punched him.

So naturally Toddie started to howl. And my mother gave my father another smirky look.

About thirty seconds later, Megamouth's voice was all sweet: "Tah-dee — come over he-ere a minute. Look what's over here."

"Tell her you can see good from here," I said to Toddie. "I can see good from here," he said. She punched him again. Howl. Smirky look.

Next time she called "Tah-dee," she was grinning over a stick of cherry licorice. She held it out, Toddie reached for it, she pulled it back. He kept reaching, she kept pulling back. Like a cobra — Valducci would have been proud — I flashed my hand out and snatched the licorice. I gave it to Toddie and he started chomping away on it. Suddenly — I don't know how she did it — *her* hand flashed out and snatched the licorice right out of his mouth. So that's how she finally got Toddie: dangling the chewed-up licorice stick until he climbed down from me and went over to her.

And all this happened before we even got out of town.

Give my father credit: he didn't give up. He kept gabbing with everybody, pointing out fascinating points of interest. "That's the hill I used to sled down when I was a kid. . . . That's where my first girlfriend used to live. . . ." Fascinating. No wonder people buy refrigerators from him — it's the only way to shut him up.

When we got out to the country, he was even worse: "Look, Toddie — moo-cow, moo-cow." And Toddie would jump to whichever lap was closer to the moo-cow, and my father would go "Mooooo" and Toddie would go "Mooooo" and I would go "Baaaarf." After a while my father stopped announcing the animals by name. He would just go "Moooo" or "Oinnnk" or "Baaaa" or "Quack-quack." And of course Toddie had to do likewise. We were a regular rolling barnyard.

Then they sang "Old MacDonald Had a Farm." By "they" I mean my father and Toddie. They must have gone through thirty or forty verses. It came to a halt when my father sang, "And on the farm he had some platypuses," and my mother screamed, "STOP!"

We pulled in at a place called Barney's Barn. It was like a flea market. People selling stuff at tables. Mostly junk. I took one look and was ready to head back to the car. Then I figured as long as I was there, maybe I should pick up a cheap birthday present for Sara. I looked through doorknobs and rusty old tools and World War II helmets and candles. Then I came to a table with jewelry. Most of it looked pretty old and ratty. I was ready to give up, when a bracelet caught my eye. It was a silver chain with a fancy silver letter hanging from it. The letter was *J*.

I knew right away I had to have it. I was meant to buy that bracelet and give it to Jennifer. The tag on it said eight dollars. I told the lady all I had was five. "Take it for five," she said. What else could she say? She was putty in the hands of fate.

When we left Barney's Barn, we rode around some more. By the time we pulled into a place to eat, it was the middle of the afternoon. "I wanted everybody to get good and hungry," my father said, "because now we can all make pigs of ourselves." The restaurant was attached to a farm. It was smorgasbord style. Everybody paid the same price; then you could eat all you wanted.

Megamouth and Toddie were the biggest pigs. Megamouth went back to the food tables seven times. Toddie was even more sickening. He ate three helpings of roast beef, three pieces of chocolate cream pie, two dishes of ice cream, five snowflake rolls with apple butter, and a pickle. I ate okay, but probably not my money's worth. I just wasn't real hungry. I kept touching the bracelet in my pocket. Once, I went to the bathroom just for a chance to look at it.

It was nearly five o'clock when we left the restaurant. I figured we would head home then. Wrong. My father decided that since it was almost Thanksgiving, he wanted to share with his happy little family something he hadn't had since he was a kid: fresh pumpkin pie made with a real pumpkin. My mother tried to tell him canned pumpkin tasted better, but it was a losing cause. "Okay," she finally sighed, "find a pumpkin."

So we started riding all over the place looking for a pumpkin. Now I was getting a little nervous. My father noticed. "What time's your date?" he called back.

Megamouth pounced. "Woo-woo! Muscles got a big date! Who's it with, Muscles? Betty Barbell?"

"It's not a date," I informed my father. "Just a party. It starts at eight."

"No problem," he says, "no problem."

The sun was dipping behind the hills. We couldn't find a pumpkin place. My father stopped at a farmhouse to ask. They gave him directions that took him about an hour to write down. The sky was red.

By the time we found the pumpkin place, it was dark. Actually, the place was a cider mill, with a wagon full of pumpkins outside. So, did we just grab a pumpkin and head for home? Oh no. We had to go into the place ("Smell that! Smell those apples!" swooned my father) and look around at the homemade pies and cider and wooden crafts.

The cider was being made in a pit. There was a railing around it, and you could stand there and look down at this big wooden press that was mashing out the cider into a wooden vat. A man was dumping bushels of apples onto a conveyer belt that led to the press. I have to explain all that because of what happened next.

My mother was looking over the donuts when Toddie

tugged on her sleeve. "Mom, I think I gotta throw —" Before he got to "up," his hand shot to his mouth, his body sort of rippled, and his eyes bugged out. "Wait!" my mother yelled. She grabbed him by the arm and started jerking him around, this way, that way, desperate. Then she spotted the railing and jerked him over to it just in time for Toddie to pop his head between the two rails and barf, smack-dab into the cider vat. The apple-dumper man below just stood there at first, watching the barf come down till it splattered in the vat. Then he let out a curse I didn't think country people knew and lunged for a button on the wall. The conveyer belt and the apple press suddenly stopped. Then he started frantically yanking out stuff and shutting off other stuff, all the time cursing and glaring up at the railing.

By then the only one at the railing was Megamouth, and the more she laughed, the louder the apple-dumper cursed. Meanwhile, Toddie and my mother were outside, and my father was talking to the cashier. Here's how it went:

FATHER. Uh, excuse me. Is the manager in?

CASHIER. Not just now. Can I help you?

FATHER. Well, uh, something, uh, unusual — unusual — just happened.

CASHIER. Oh?

FATHER. Yes. Uh, my son — my young son — just, uh, got a little sick.

CASHIER. Oh?

FATHER. Vomited. In the, uh, apple cider, uh, vat, uh.

CASHIER. Oh!

FATHER. Yes.

CASHIER [*pointing to pit*]. There? *In* the vat?

FATHER. Yes, uh, at least I believe so. [*Calling to me*] Greg, it was *in* the vat, wasn't it? [*I nodded*]

CASHIER. Well, uh, I don't think I know just what to do.

FATHER. I suppose I don't either. Too bad the manager isn't here.

CASHIER. Yes, it is.

FATHER. I guess the cider in the vat must be spoiled now, hm? Safe to say that?

CASHIER. Mm. I guess it's safe. To say.

FATHER. Lot of cider in there.

CASHIER. Mm.

FATHER. [*Pauses, looks all around, smiles, looks at watch, takes out wallet, pulls little white card out of wallet*] Well, look, since the manager's not here, why don't you give him this card, my business card, and have him call me. I'll be glad to pay for anything.

CASHIER. All right. Thank you.

FATHER [*clapping, rubbing his hands together*]. All right. Fine. Say, how's your refrigerator working these days?

CASHIER [*taken by surprise*]. Oh — fine, thank you.

FATHER. Washing machine?

CASHIER. Fine.

FATHER. Well [*points to card*], stop in and see me. I'll see that you're taken care of. [*Walking away*] That goes for your manager too.

We left then, but Megamouth kept coming up with reasons why we should go back, so I would be late for the party. First she tried to tell my father that barf is lighter than apple cider, so he should go back and tell them to just skim the barf off the top; that way he wouldn't have to repay them for a whole vatful. Then she reminded him that he forgot to get what he went there for: his pumpkin. He slowed down to turn around, but my mother said, very calmly and firmly, "Do not stop this car. Do not turn back. Keep driving."

But then, finally, we did have to stop — we ran out of gas. I jumped out, took my father's wallet, and ran halfway back across the state till I came to an old grocery store with a gasoline pump outside.

Well, to make a long, *long* story short, it was almost ten o'clock when I got to the party. Sara opened the door. "Where have you been?"

"Sorry," I said. "I was out with my parents. We just got back." I was trying not to pant from running.

"This late?"

"Yeah."

Sara kept saying things to me and I kept saying things back, but I wasn't paying much attention. Behind her the party was going on: records, laughing, popcorn sailing. Poff and Valducci were there, and others I knew, but I wasn't paying attention to them either. Because sitting on the arm of an easy chair by the fireplace, slouched back, talking to two girls, was Jennifer Wade.

I felt something on my arm. Sara, tugging. "Greg, wake up. Give me your jacket."

Then, like a dream: I was taking off my jacket, and there was a car horn in the night outside, and I was clenching my fist, and Jennifer Wade was getting up from the arm of the chair and she was coming toward me. She was smiling. She was wearing a jacket, lavender, with white fur.

She came right up. She spoke. "That's my dad, Sara. Gotta go."

"Already?"

"Yeah. The pits, huh?"

"I'll say. Boy, some party. This goob gets here late and you're leaving early."

Jennifer turned, looked at me, smiled. The most beautiful smile I ever saw. "Well," she said, laying her fingers on my arm, "at least you *have* a date."

They both laughed then, and Jennifer was out the door, calling back, "Happy birthday!" And the door closed.

My arm, where she touched it, sent a small, sweet bolt of lightning to the center of my heart.

Megin

IT WAS late in the first half of our final game. We were smearing Huntington Valley, 6 to 0, so that's why I was on the bench along with the other first-stringers. Sue Ann was in the game. She was going for a loose ball and was just ready to scoop it up when she got hammered by this big gorilla of a girl from Huntington Valley. I mean, the gorilla didn't just foul Sue Ann, she practically killed her. The way she swung her stick, she wasn't going for the ball at all, but for Sue Ann's legs. The stick caught Sue Ann across the shins. Sue Ann went down like a rock, screaming so loud you'd never have known she was on the other side of the field.

I don't remember leaving the bench. I don't remember crossing the field. I only remember slinging my stick at the gorilla — and the look of surprise on her face as she turned and saw me flying through the air at her. I think I landed pretty much on her face, and big and blubbery as she was, she made a good cushion when we hit the deck. Before she knew what was happening, I jumped up and stomped on both her shins. She howled. I stomped on them again. She howled again. Then we were on the ground rolling and wrestling, and pretty soon the whole Huntington Valley team was on us. I felt like a blob of toothpaste being squeezed through a rolled-up tube. I could hear whistles, and coaches' and teachers' voices. I could hardly breathe, mostly because something soft was plumped against my face. So I bit it. Somebody screamed bloody murder. Then the load was lightening from above and I was being pried from the others. My coach practically had me in a hammerlock as she steered me back across the field. I looked over my shoulder. The gorilla was standing in front of her coach, clutching her left boob with both hands and bawling, "She *bit* me!"

When we reached the bench, the coach spun me around and grabbed me by the shoulders and started shaking me. "Tofer, what in God's name do you think you're doing?"

"What am *I* doing?" I yelled. "Ask that gorilla over there what *she's* doing!" I pointed to Sue Ann, who was limping off the field with her arms draped over two other players. "Ask Sue Ann!"

She shook me some more. "You are *not* judge and jury around here, Tofer! That girl was called for a foul. The referee is in charge of this game. Not you. This is organized athletics. Not the street. We follow the rules here. There's such a thing as sportsmanship."

"Yeah? Tell that to that gorilla!"

"I'm telling it to you!"

"Well, I'm telling you!" I wrenched out of her grip. "I quit!"

I walked away. The coach kept calling my name, but I never stopped, I never looked back.

* * *

Quitting lacrosse was no big deal. What did I miss? The last half of the last game. And anyway, lacrosse was only something for me to do while I was waiting for the first ice — and ice hockey.

Meanwhile, it turned out that Mr. MacWilliams hadn't kicked me off stage crew forever. When I asked him about joining up again, he threw his hands in the air and went, "Praise be! Where have you been, woman? The peace and quiet around here's been driving me crazy Go. Grab a hammer. Cause some trouble."

I'm starting to like Mr. MacWilliams.

I got back on stage crew just in time. Juliet — Zoe Miranda got the part, of course — and Romeo were practicing their first love-scene. It goes like this: Juliet comes out of McDonald's, heaves bag of trash into Dipsy Dumpster, hears howl from inside. Head pops out of Dumpster. It's Romeo. He's hiding from the Burger King boss, who's looking for someone to clean the bathroom. So, as soon as their eyes meet, they fall in love. That's when they sing their first duet: "Some Enchanted Dipsy Dumpster." Then they kiss.

But the best part was happening offstage. Valducci, the light-man, has a thing for Zoe. He can't stand the love scene. So each time Romeo leans down from the Dumpster to kiss Zoe, something strange always seems to happen with the lights. Like all the lights — footlights, overheads, spot — will go on at once. Or the colored lights will go crazy. Or the spotlight will zoom like some wacko trapped horsefly all over the auditorium. Mr. MacWilliams keeps yelling "Val-dooo-cci!" but it doesn't do much good.

Sue Ann and I had a ball, mimicking the whole thing behind the scenery. I stood on a ladder and played Romeo; Sue Ann was Juliet. We were really going great one day, especially during the duet, moving our mouths and throwing out our hands and all. A couple times squeaks slipped out of my mouth, but nothing happened, so we kept going. Then, on a long high note, I accidentally let out a super-squeak. I could hear Mr. MacWilliams shout, "Stop! Halt!" Then: "Megin! Tofer! Out here!"

Sue Ann was red-faced and clamping her mouth. I went out. Mr. MacWilliams was in his usual place, middle of the third row. Romeo and Juliet were glaring at me.

"What's the matter?" I said.

"Megin," called Mr. MacWilliams, "since you seem to know the part so well, why don't you take Miss Miranda's place for a minute. I'm sure we would all appreciate seeing how a real Juliet plays the part."

"Okay," I said (much to Mr. MacWilliams's surprise), and I strolled on over to the Dumpster. Zoe Miranda stepped aside with a big bow and a sweep of her arm. The other kids clapped. The rest of the stage crew came out to watch.

Sometimes I do crazy things, so I wasn't totally shocked to find myself in the center of the stage ready to play Juliet. What did shock me, though, was that I was allowing myself to do it with Jeremy Bach, who was Romeo. Bad enough that he's a ninth-grader, but he's also a total creep and a goober. He thinks every girl is in love with him.

"All right!" called Mr. MacWilliams. "Music!"

Somebody turned on the tape recorder. Jeremy Romeo hesitated, but I jumped right into it, really belting it out. The place went wild. Clapping. Whistles. Hoots. Comments. ("Who taughtcha ta sing? Kermit the Frog?" ... "Let *her* play Romeo!" ... "Kill it with a stick!") Jeremy Romeo joined in then and we really socked it. I tried to catch the look on Mr. MacWilliams's face, but I couldn't see, because the spotlight was on me again. When we finished there was another round of comments and hoots. But the comments and hoots were outlouded by the clapping and whistles.

Then Jeremy Romeo was leaning down for the big kiss He was kneeling on a table; we didn't have the Dumpster reinforced yet. I saw his face coming at me, his eyes closing in. He was leaning, leaning, his hands were on my shoulders. I let his face get closer. His mouth went funny, his eyes shut. The rest was easy: I took one step back and — Ka-ploppo! — he fell to the floor on his goober face. Howls. Wild cheering. Stomping feet. Stage lights going crazy. I bowed to Zoe Miranda and made my grand exit.

Morning after morning I woke up and looked out my window — no ice. It was December. What was going on? My skates, my hockey stick, my puck — they were all in the corner, waiting.

If the ice had come sooner, probably I wouldn't have gone to the party. But on the day Mr. MacWilliams made the announcement, December 5, the temperature outside was sixty-two degrees. It was after rehearsal. He called everyone to the stage and said, "Ladies and gentlemen, our Juliet, Zoe Miranda, would like you all to know that you are invited to a party on Thursday evening from six till eight. Miss Miranda says if you have ice skates, by all means bring them. The party will be at the Skatium."

I boggled at Sue Ann. "Did he say what I think he said?"

"Yeah. An ice-skating party."

It was true. Zoe's parents, who must be millionaires, had rented the Skatium rink for two hours Thursday night. I didn't want to be the only one there with a hockey stick, so I checked around and found three other players — all boys (two in the cast, one in the crew). "Just bring your stick," I told each of them. "I got the puck."

When I saw the rink, I wanted to laugh and cry at the same time, it was so beautiful. I'm a lake rat, not a rink rat, and I almost never get to the Skatium. I could hardly lace up my skates, my hands were so nervous.

The ice was smooth as glass. I just went around and around — push off–glide, push off–glide — almost with my eyes shut, just soaking it up, just feeling the ice beneath my blades, just being where I belong.

When I finally came out of my daze, I started to notice the party. Besides the play people, other friends of Zoe were there, plus a bunch of grown-ups. Off to the side there was a long table with a row of silver dishes with steam coming out, and two tall cakes with white icing.

Most of the kids were dressed pretty much like me — jeans and sweaters and stuff. A couple girls, Zoe's groupies, had on teeny-weeny skating skirts and tights, like they were in the Ice Follies or something. Then there was Zoe: shimmering light green tutu, silver tights, white skate shoes, and a *fur* jacket. Only Zoe.

Well, I had business to take care of. I took my puck out, dropped it to the ice, and flipped it into the butt of one of the boys with a stick. The fun was on! We zipped around the rink, dodging in and out of the others, chasing each other, firing passes back and forth across the ice. I was in heaven.

After a long spring and summer without hockey, I was gradually getting back the feel of it. At first the puck seemed kind of mushy on my stick, but then the puck started to pop — *pop!* — off the stick. Once it popped a little too good, I guess. I was passing the puck to a guy across the ice, and it just sprang off my stick, rising off the ice —

one of the best slap shots I ever hit—passing over the flailing stick of the kid, passing under the chin of Zoe Miranda's mother, and never stopping till it sank into one of the tall white cakes.

In two seconds Zoe was making a beeline for me. "Tofer—"

"I know, I know," I said. "No more hockey."

She skated right up to me and glared, hands on hips, lips tight. Finally she turned and glided off. But I wasn't finished. Quickly I reached into my pocket, dropped my substitute puck to the ice, and called, "Hey, Zoe!" As she was turning around, my stick was already flashing forward; as she gaped goggle-eyed, the puck was halfway there; before the scream could leave her throat she got caught smack in the face by the puck—which looks exactly like a regular puck but is actually a spongy Nerf puck.

It bounced off her nose and fluttered to the ice at her feet. She kept staring at it, her hand still frozen halfway to her face. Then she did something I never expected: she started to laugh. She picked up the Nerf puck and glided over to me and bounced it off *my* nose, and for the next five minutes we were both laughing so hard we almost wobbled off our skate blades.

"Y'know," she said when she could finally speak again, "I'm glad you did that stuff to Jeremy Bach at rehearsal the other day."

"Me too," I said. "He's such a goob. How can you stand to kiss him?"

"I can't. But he can't stand me either."

"How's that?"

"Before every rehearsal I rub my lips with garlic!"

We roared. My own laughter hit me harder than a body check. I fell down.

Then she showed me how to do an axel, and I showed her how to hit a slap shot. She was too dainty, but I told her she was good for a beginner. Then suddenly she looked behind me and shoved the stick into my hands. "Here, you do it." I turned. Who was heading toward us — or should I say toward *her* — but the one and only karate klunkhead, Eddie Valducci. He had a cup of hot apple cider in each hand, and since he's a rotten skater to start with, he was herking and jerking all over the place. Even though I was standing next to Zoe, he never saw me. I waited till he got to point-blank range. The shot was perfect, the rest was even better: the look on his face, the cider flying, his skates flying, his butt crashing to the ice, two girls skating off practically dying of laughter.

Greg

At least you have a date.

Jennifer Wade's words had been spoken to Sara Bellamy, but it was my brain they burned into. What exactly did she mean by them? Why did her fingers touch my arm when she spoke them? Would Leo Borlock, the lovelorn expert, have the answers? I almost called him.

I wished so many things. I wished she hadn't left early. I wished I had turned my arm a little so she could feel my vein. I wished I had found some excuse to follow her outside so I could say to her: "Date? Is that what Sara told you? Ha-ha. I'm not her date. She just invited me to her party. Actually I'm here by myself. I'm not attached to anybody."

But those things didn't happen, so all I was left with were her words: *At least you have a date.*

I thought and thought about those words, and the more I thought about them, the clearer they became. She was saying a lot more than it seemed at first. She was saying, "I'm alone." And, "I'm lonely." And, "I wish I had someone."

And (remember the fingers), "I wish I had someone like you, Greg."

It all came together for me on the first snow day of the year. The snow was already a foot high when I woke up, and it was still coming down. I turned on my radio. Sure enough, all the city schools were closed, and most of the ones in the suburbs too. Then the announcer started reading off the numbers of the closed schools. First I heard my school's number called, then Conestoga's, hers: "eleven fifty-five." Just hearing her number gave me a warm feeling.

I turned off the radio. I sat on the edge of the bed with my blankets wrapped around me and just stared out the window. The snowflakes fell fat and slow, and I could actually see individual flakes land and collapse on the little curved drift on my windowsill. Were they landing on Jennifer's windowsill too? Of course. The snow was falling on her house as well as mine, heaping silently upon it, huddling, cuddling, snuggling around it, closing over it, over her . . .

I jumped up, reached for the *J* bracelet. It was time. Right now. I found a little box, stuffed some cotton into it, then the bracelet, then a little slip of paper: "From Greg Tofer. No one *has* to be alone." I wrapped it, addressed it, got dressed, left the house, and headed for the post office. Hardly anything was plowed or shoveled yet, the snow was up to my boot tops, and the post office was a mile away, but I didn't care. I would have walked across Siberia.

When I reached the post office, I had to wait ten minutes for them to open up. Then I put the box on the counter. "I want to send this," I told the postman.

"Okay," he said, putting it on a scale. "How do you want it to go?"

"By mail," I said.

His eyes shifted to me. He nodded. "By mail. Okay. *How* by mail? First class? Third class?"

"First class."

"First class. Costs more, you know."

"That's okay."

"Insured?"

"Huh?"

"Want it insured?"

"What's that?"

"If it doesn't reach its destination, you're covered."

"What's that mean?"

"You get the amount of money it's insured for." He took the box from the scale. "What's it worth?"

How do you answer a question like that? "About a million dollars," I said.

He grinned. "Wha'd you pay for it?"

"Five dollars."

"I guess it doesn't need insurance." He hit the box twice with a rubber stamp. "Two-ten."

I gave him the money. He slapped stamps on the box and pitched it into a big, dirty gray sack. All of a sudden I wished I never had brought it to the post office. I wished I were walking the ten miles to Conestoga. Get there by nightfall, slip it into her mailbox. "Say — uh —" I said. He looked up. "Is it gonna get there? I mean for sure?"

He gave a thumbs-up sign. "It'll get there." As I was leaving he called, "If I have to carry it myself!"

I charged outside, made sure nobody was looking, and went a little nutso. I whooped and yahooed and flung snow around and just generally made an idiot of myself.

On the way back I picked up Poff and Valducci. In spite of the snow, Homestead Lake wasn't frozen over yet, so ice hockey was out. That left sledding. Poff didn't have a sled. Valducci did. His sled was the lid of his neighbor's metal trash can. He stomped on the handle till it was flat. I picked up my sled too, a red plastic sheet.

We headed for the park, and the best sledding hill around. Sledders were already there, and before long, half the kids in town were zooming down the slope. What a great day! Racing. Hijacking sleds. Snowball fights. Snowball *wars*. (Somebody got a big cardboard box and made a sled-tank.)

The little kids, the snowman makers, sometimes they're so dumb. In the early part of the day they made their snowmen at the bottom of the hill. Now, did they really think some big kid sledders would not "accidentally" go plowing through them? So dumb.

So they wised up and started making their snowmen at the top of the hill. Unfortunately, that wasn't much better — not with Valducci around. Two little kids had just finished making a snowman — I mean a really great snowman, hat and all — when Valducci spotted it. Next thing you know, he's hugging and kissing it and moaning, "Oh Zoe, my Zoe, why oh why are you so cold to me?" (Zoe is the name of Valducci's latest. She's from California, looks like a walking jewelry store, and is only in seventh grade. I keep telling him he's robbing the cradle. He tells me he's tired of biting into those tough, gristly old ninth-grade birds.) Then Valducci backed off — "Hey, you're not Zoe!" He high-kicks the snowman's hat off, then the carrot nose. Then he karate-chops the arms off, then he punches the head off, then he takes care of the rest with a flying two-legged kick. The sight of that, plus the look on the little kids' faces — I don't think I ever saw anything so funny and so pitiful at the same time.

Valducci finally notices the little kids. He jumps up, grabs the snowman hat, puts it on, jams the carrot into his mouth, and stands there trying to look like Frosty. The kids weren't impressed. Then, as if somebody had given a signal, all three of us started rolling snow, and in ten minutes that snowman was bigger and better than before, and the little kids were laughing again and sailing down the hill on Poff's back, which is so wide the kids rode on it side by side instead of double-decker.

Plenty of girls were there. Funny thing about girls in the snow: with their hats and scarves and boots and mittens and all, at a distance, through your own snow-breath, almost any one of them can look like whatever girl you want her to be. I swore I saw Jennifer Wade a dozen times — flinging snow, running, screaming. I kept thinking maybe, maybe she'd come back to the hill where she used to sled.

One time, after I'd started back in the trees and flopped on my sled right at the crest of the hill for the longest possible ride down, my breath popped out with a grunt as somebody landed on my back. I barely managed to keep on course. I knew it wasn't Poff. I figured it was Valducci. Then, about halfway down the hill and really moving, a pair of bright red mittens appeared in front of my face and closed over my eyes. *Jennifer!* I thought for a split second. Then a voice said, "Guess who, *monsieur?*" Sara.

She reached out, jerked the front of the sled, and we both lurched into the snow and went rolling down the rest of the hill. We came to a stop at somebody's feet. Valducci's.

"Well, well —," he leered down at us — "looks like we got a coupla holy rollers here."

I pulled Valducci's legs from under him; before he hit the ground, Sara was on him with a faceful of snow.

From then on, it was a bunch of us ninth-graders, boys

and girls, just generally messing around and going snow-crazy. I guess the funniest part was the double- and triple- and even quadruple-decker plunging sled fights, kind of bumper cars in the snow. Or you might say musical sleds, the way the girls kept switching the boys whose backs they flopped on. Except for Sara. She always seemed to be on me.

Once, after tumbling to a stop at the bottom of the hill, Sara held me as I started to get up. She was giving me a sly grin. "I was wondering whether to forgive you for not giving me a birthday present," she said. I started stammering out some excuses, but she cut me short. "But then, silly me, I realized you had a birthday present for me all along." She winked and patted my lips with her mitten. "You were just waiting for the right moment to give it to me, weren't you?" She pulled up her hood and closed her eyes and tilted her face close to mine.

A thousand questions went through my mind. The loudest was: *What if somebody tells Jennifer Wade about this?* I got mad thinking about that, mad at Sara. Maybe *she* didn't mind people thinking we were tight, but did she ever ask me? She inched closer, her eyes still closed. "Hey," she whispered, "don't bother wrapping it." The sly grin was gone from her lips; they were parted slightly. I had to get out of this, fast. I quick gave her a peck; not even that really — a half-peck. Then I jumped up and slung some snow at her. "Can't catch me!" I yelled and started running.

"Your sled!" she called.

"Who cares!"

"Okay — you asked for it!" She screamed and scooped up snow and started after me.

I ran up the hill and into the trees. I ran and ran.

Through the picnic grove, past the snow-seated swings, sliding board, past the pavilion, the tennis courts, the softball field, the Little League field. I didn't look back. I could hear her voice, her yelling. I was surprised at how long she stayed close. But then she began to fall back, her voice became fainter, and I could tell, I could tell without even looking, that she couldn't believe I wasn't letting her catch me. Finally, when I was out of the park, onto the streets, I stopped and turned around. She was gone.

For the next few days I didn't have to avoid Sara. She avoided me. I mean, when she saw me in the halls and classrooms she might look at me and give me a puzzled kind of smile, but she didn't try to talk to me. Until Friday morning. Before homeroom. I was at my locker getting books when I heard behind me, "I was talking to a friend of yours last night."

Until I turned around I wasn't sure it was Sara. Her voice was so different. There was something different about her face too. Why was I having trouble swallowing? "Who's that?" I smiled.

"Jennifer Wade." She did not smile back.

"Oh yeah?"

"Yeah. You know, Jennifer with a *J*? The kind of *J* you find on bracelets?"

I turned back to my locker, started looking through some notebooks. The bell rang.

"Creep," she said.

I heard her walking away.

Megin

IT WAS ONLY a little after noontime on Saturday, so I never expected to find my mother doing her surviving then — and especially not *there*. But she was.

Sue Ann and I had just done our Christmas shopping, and we were ready to dump our loads in my room. Sue Ann was ahead of me. Just inside the doorway she suddenly stopped and turned. "Your mother," she whispered. "She's sleeping on your bed."

I looked. It was my mother, all right; on her back, straight, hands folded over chest. I pushed Sue Ann into the room. "She's not sleeping."

Sue Ann went a couple steps, then froze. She gawked at my mother for a while, then she snapped around to me. Her face was white, her eyes were big as hockey pucks. Her hand went to her mouth. "Oh God! Oh *God!*"

I started laughing. "She's not dead, you peanut brain." I dumped my bags on the bed at my mother's feet. "She's just in a trance. I told you how she hypnotizes herself. She's surviving."

Sue Ann was petrified. I grabbed her and pulled. She wouldn't take a step, so I just pulled on her arms and her feet came sliding across the floor on a pair of notebooks. (My room was back to normal.) I dragged her up real close. "Look, now, see? She's breathing. See her chest move."

"I don't see it."

I sighed. "You're hopeless." I grabbed her hand and led her to a chair and sat her down.

I opened my bags and laid out my presents. By the time I was through, my mother was half covered with them. There were things for her (slippers), my father (aftershave lotion), Toddie (Road Runner coloring book), Jackie (earrings), Emilie (leg warmers), and, of course, Sue Ann (mittens). I held up the things for Sue Ann to see (except the mittens). "Who're they for?" she said when I held up the leg warmers.

"Friend of mine," I said.

"Who?"

"Emilie."

"Emilie? Emilie who?"

"Bain."

"Emilie Bain? Who's that? She go to our school?"

"Nope."

"She live around here?"

"Yep."

"What school does she go to?"

"She doesn't."

While Sue Ann was being silently baffled on the chair, I tried putting one of the slippers on my mother's foot. It fit.

"Did it ever occur to you," I said, "that maybe something could happen in my life that you wouldn't know about?" I felt rotten as soon as I said that. Sure enough, Sue Ann's eyes were starting to water up. "I'm sorry," I said. "I didn't mean it that way. Emilie is eighty-nine years old. She lives at Beechwood Manor." I pointed to the picture. "That's her."

She looked, still baffled. "Is that a real rabbit?"

"Yeah," I laughed, "it's real."

When I finished showing Sue Ann all the presents, she said, "Where's Greg's?"

I almost choked. "Grosso's? You crazy? I don't get him one."

"You got Toddie something."

"That's different. He's cute."

"Does Greg give you something?"

"You kidding? I wouldn't take it even if he did."

Then Sue Ann climbed onto her pulpit. "Well," she said, "that's not very Christmassy."

"What do you mean by that?"

"Well, you're supposed to have goodwill toward *all* men."

"Where does it say toward all donkeys?"

I never got an answer. Sue Ann squeaked, her whole body stiffened, her eyes got foggy. I looked behind me— my mother's eyes were open. Other than that, she hadn't moved. She's always like that for the first couple seconds after coming out of it. Looks like a vampire ready to rise. Then I realized: the slippers, they were out! I quick grabbed them and shoved them in a bag, just as my mother blinked and started to look around. When she saw me and Sue Ann, she closed her eyes again.

I shook her. "Mom. C'mon now. You gotta get up."

"I don't want to."

"Mo-om." I pulled her legs over the side of the bed and sat her up. Her eyes were still shut. I pried them open. "Mom, snap out of it."

She gave a little smile. "It's so nice where I was."

"Yeah, well, it's nice here too. And anyway, what are you doing surviving now? It's not even three o'clock. And on my bed?"

"Christmas."

"Huh?"

"Christmas is one of the worst times. Some days I can't wait till three."

I looked at Sue Ann. My eyes said, See? I told you. Her eyes said, *Amazing.* I pulled my mother to her feet and steered her out of the room.

When Sue Ann left, I wrapped Emilie's present and went out. Snow flurries were blowing. The air was freezing. I stopped at Dunkin' Donuts for a french cruller. Jackie wasn't there, and neither was anybody else who was nice, so I had to pay for one.

Emilie is just like me: no self-control. As soon as she spied the present, she snatched it and tore it open. Even though she made all sorts of surprised and happy noises, I knew she didn't have the slightest idea of what I'd given her. "They're leg warmers," I told her. "You're gonna need them when we play hockey."

"Oouuu goody," she giggled. "Can I wear them now?"

"Sure." I put them on her.

She pointed to her pillow. A present sat there. "That's yours," she said.

I ripped it open. It was a T-shirt. It said:

I AM
A
GRETZKY
GIRL

I shrieked. "Emilie, I love it! Where'd you get it?"

"Oh," she said, "I sent my brother out for it. I told him to go to one of those places that put the words on."

I tore my coat off and pulled the shirt on over my sweater. I looked in the mirror. "It's beautiful. Gorgeous." I gave her a hug and she kissed me, and then we just sort of strutted around the room for a while, her in her leg warmers, me in my Gretzky shirt, admiring ourselves.

Then we decorated her wheelchair. We hung some tinsel from the arms — lots of it. Then we made two red-and-green paper chains and threaded them through the wheel spokes. We tested the chains in the hallway. The faster we went, the neater they looked — a red-green blur.

Emilie had to go to dinner then — "Ugh!" she said — so I waited in her room. "Ugh!" she said when she came back. "I hate that stuff they feed me. You have any more crullers with you?"

"No," I said.

"Check your pockets."

I checked. "Sorry."

"Well then," she said, "let's go get some."

I thought she was kidding. She wasn't. She had me get

her coat out of the closet and wrap her in blankets. I put three pairs of socks on her feet, then her warmest slippers. I was glad for the leg warmers. Last of all, I gave her my hat. It's red-and-white candy-cane stripes with a big fuzzball on top. I pulled it way down over her ears.

Outside, it was even colder than before. "You warm enough?" I asked her, but she wasn't listening. She was looking, all around, her eyes wide open, like she was seeing the world for the first time. "Look," she said, "snow!"

"It's just flurries," I told her.

"And the lights! Aren't they beautiful! You didn't tell me it was so beautiful out here. Let's go see the lights. All of them."

I laughed. "Emilie, we can't see them all. It's a big town, you know." But she was already rolling herself down the sidewalk.

She didn't say another word about donuts. We went up one street and down the next. All along the way, Emilie kept saying, "Look at that one! . . . Look at that one!" Once or twice each block she would go, *"That's* the best one!" And then, a couple houses later: *"That's* the best!"

After a while we started singing carols. Emilie is amazing. She knows all the verses of all the songs. She kept getting mad at me because I only knew the first verses. We must have been pretty loud, because every once in a while somebody would come to the front door and smile at us and listen.

Then I heard a sound that was *really* music to my ears: car tires spinning. I couldn't see where it was coming from, but somebody was having a hard time. The tires were screaming. I jumped about ten feet in the air. "Ice!" Emilie looked at me like I was crazy. I grabbed her shoulders.

"Ice, Emilie! Ice! Ice! The lake's freezing over! There's gonna be ice! There's gonna be hockey!"

Emilie brought her hands from under the blankets and held my face in them. "Let's go."

"The lake? Now?"

"Now."

I didn't need any more arm twisting; Homestead Lake was only about five blocks away. When we got there, the floodlights were off, so I knew the ice wasn't ready yet. When the ice is thick enough, the lights stay on till nine each night.

The lake isn't far from the sidewalk. We could see it dimly in the street light. I left Emilie and went to check things out. I lowered my foot slowly over the edge—it stopped. Ice all right. I put on a little pressure. The ice held. A little more pressure. I heard cracking. I went back to Emilie. "Yep, it's ice. Couple more days now."

I told her what it would be like: all the kids—choosing sides—wild, screaming games—the nets—the practice backboard—the fence at the edge of the lighted area, so nobody will go into the middle of the lake, where the ice is thin. Emilie was looking at me, smiling. "You really love that ice, don't you?"

"Yeah," I chuckled, "guess so."

Then, just looking at her, I knew it was the right time to do something that had been on my mind for weeks. I pulled out a little white card and gave it to her. I was never so nervous in my life. "Can you read it in this light?" I asked her.

She held it out, kept moving it around to get the best light. "I think so. I'll give it a try."

It was a regular business-type card, like my father has, with real printing.

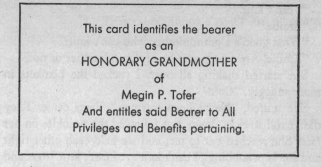

This card identifies the bearer
as an
HONORARY GRANDMOTHER
of
Megin P. Tofer
And entitles said Bearer to All
Privileges and Benefits pertaining.

She was taking a year to read it. The longer I stood there, the more I knew I had blown it. When I couldn't stand the silence any longer, I started explaining. I told her I'd never had a real grandmother, because they both died before I was born. I told her that my mother had helped me with the wording on the card, and that a shop teacher in school had done the printing for me. I told her she didn't have to take it seriously.

She said something, but I couldn't make it out. I knelt down. Now I could see her face. Her lip was quivering. Her eyes rose to mine, fell back to the card. "I can't be a grandmother. I don't know how."

I laughed. "You don't have to know how. You just *be* one."

"I don't cook good."

"So what?"

"Grandmothers are great cooks. Everybody loves to eat there. All my soft-boiled eggs come out too hard."

"I'll give you cooking lessons. Soon as I get them in school."

"I hate rocking chairs."

"Emilie."

"I can't knit."

"Emilie."

"What good's a grandmother who can't knit?"

"Emilie! Are you gonna be my grandmother or not?"

She started shaking all over. I tucked the blankets in more snuggly. "Cold?"

She sniffed, "Never been warmer." Tears came. They didn't roll straight down, but followed the wrinkles on her face. She reached out to me, and we held each other tight and she kept sobbing "I can't knit . . . I can't knit" over and over in the snow flurries under the streetlight by Homestead Lake.

Greg

Dear Greg,
      *Thank you for the bracelet. It was so
nice of you to send it to me ... and just in
time for Christmas! Well, thank you again.*
                              Sincerely,
                              Jennifer Wade

P.S.
Merry Christmas!

A THOUSAND. That's how many times I read the letter over and over in my room. I've never seen such beautiful handwriting. And the way she said things, it was like she was right next to me, whispering in my ear.

I just wanted to stay there the whole day and read it *ten* thousand times, but Christmas was only two days away and I had to go shopping at the mall with Poff and Valducci. With the letter in my pocket, I floated out of the house. I left my mother and Toddie and Megamouth behind, fighting in the living room over how to decorate the tree. They could hang bananas on it for all I cared.

At the mall I got a portable car vacuum cleaner for my father, a bracelet for my mother, and a Road Runner coloring book for Toddie.

Valducci has a gigantic family, so he got a whole lot of little things, mostly packs of Life Savers. Then he really got stumped. He wanted to get something for that Zoe girl, the seventh-grade flash he has the hots for. "Get her a bracelet," I told him. "With a Z on it."

"Nah," he said. "Gotta be different. Them California girls seen it all. This has gotta be one of a kind."

Poff kept drifting off by himself to get his gifts. Poff lives with his mother, just her and him. No matter what store we were in, he headed for the ladies' department.

We stopped by appliances at Sears. My father was busy telling somebody what a great Christmas present a washing machine would make. He was wearing his long, red Santa cap. The way he's so jolly, it's a wonder he doesn't wear it all year around.

Walking through the mall, I couldn't get my mind off the letter. The words kept floating through my head; the Salvation Army bells put them to music.

We were on the second-floor balcony and I was looking down when I got a surprise: Sara. She was walking into a bookstore on the lower level — with Leo Borlock, our own ninth-grade shrink. She was wearing a coat I'd never seen before, with a long powder blue scarf. I felt bad at first, but then I started to feel better. I was glad she'd decided to talk it out with Leo instead of moping at home by herself. If anybody could help her, Leo could. Broken hearts are his specialty. I also felt relief for my own sake. Because now the whole problem of what to do about Sara wasn't just mine; it was Leo's too. I felt lighter. Now I could enjoy Christmas all the way.

By the time Poff was done shopping, he had two carry bags full. All for his mother, I guess. So we were ready to leave — but no Valducci. We finally found him with Santa Claus. Waiting in line with these kiddies who came up to his waist, Valducci looked like a giant. Of course, his size was the only way you could tell the difference. He was fooling around and kicking and swiping candy canes just like the others. He was attracting as much attention as Santa Claus.

When Valducci's turn came, he climbed the steps and sat on Santa's lap. He kept grinning and whispering in Santa's ear and moving his hands in the shape of a girl's figure. You didn't have to be a genius to figure exactly *who* he wanted for Christmas. He got off Santa's lap, stopped for a minute at the photographer's table, and came cruising up to us, all proud. He held out the picture — the large size, color, him on Santa's knee, grinning at the camera. "This is it," he said. "The present I was looking for. One-of-a-kind."

When the bus let us off, we walked together for a block. We decided to meet next morning at Homestead Lake with skates and sticks. The ice was ready. Then we separated.

The world never seemed so beautiful. It was a ginger-bread town, the snow like white icing spread across the lawns, drooping from the roofs, heaped along the drive-ways. Jellybean lights framed doorways and swirled around front-yard shrubs. Trees stood black like licorice sticks against a raspberry sherbet sky.

I opened our door to the smell of grilled cheese sandwiches and the sparkling lights of our Christmas tree.

I ate dinner, but I didn't taste it. I watched a little TV,

but I didn't see it. Then I made the call, the call I had been thinking about all day, heading for all my life.

She answered. "Hello?"

"Hello? Jennifer?"

"Yes?"

"This is Greg, uh, Tofer. 'Member me?"

"Oh yeah. Hi."

"Hi. Just thought I'd, uh, give you a little call. Wanted to, uh, let you know I got your letter."

"Oh yeah, the thank-you note."

"Yeah. I, uh, it was a, uh, very nice note. Wanted to thank you for it."

"Well, you're welcome."

"Thanks."

"And thank you."

"Uh, what for?"

"The bracelet."

"Oh yeah. Guess I got a little mixed up there." I laughed. "Say, Jennifer, how's, uh, your shopping going so far?"

"Oh, okay, I guess. So far so good."

"Only one day left, y'know."

"Yeah, I know. Almost here."

"Sure is. When is it? Day after tomorrow?"

"Yep."

"Christmas. Wow." She didn't answer. It was so quiet I thought maybe the line had gone dead. Then I heard her clear her throat. I spoke up. "Yeah, Christmas — oh say, Jen, listen, speaking of Christmas, you guys have, uh, you're on vacation over there, aren't you? Till after New Year's, I mean?"

"Far as I know."

"Yeah. Thought so. Us too." More silence. No throat

clearing this time. "Yeah, well, listen, Jen. I was wondering, uh, d'you think you might like to go out someplace some night? Well, 'course, some *day* would be okay too." I laughed. "I don't know, movies or something?"

"Well, I don't know. I'm kind of pretty tied up around the holidays. We have to go visiting a lot of relatives, you know."

"Oh yeah, that's right. Me too. Christmas. Relatives. Yeah, know what you mean. Sort of, uh, be busy just about every day, I guess, huh?"

"Probably."

"Lotta relatives."

"Tons."

I laughed. "Yeah, me too." Silence. "Well, listen, just wanted to call and thank you for the letter. So — uh — thanks again."

"You're welcome."

"Okay. Bye now."

"Bye."

"Oh — Merry Christmas, Jen."

"Same to you."

"Seeya."

"Bye."

When I put the receiver down, my heart felt the weight of it.

What happened? What was going on? Until now, everything seemed to be going forward: her words at Sara's party, sending her the bracelet, her letter. Each one a step forward. Now the phone call. Was it a step forward? Backward? Anywhere? Okay, I didn't get a date with her. Right. But did she say she didn't *want* to go out with me? No. She said she *couldn't*. "Pretty tied up," she had said. Not wouldn't, couldn't. Relatives. Visiting. Christmas.

Understandable. I took out the letter. There: ". . . so nice of you to send it to me." So nice . . . so nice. And the "Merry Christmas!" With an exclamation point. Not the words, not the letter of a girl who would never want to go out with me. So why was I feeling so . . . so *what?* How *was* I feeling? Good? No, not really, to be honest. Bad? Well, a little closer maybe, but that couldn't really be it either. I mean, what was there, *exactly*, to feel bad *about?* And damn if I was going to feel bad without a pretty good reason.

Late that night I made up an excuse to leave the house. I snuck back through the basement door for my stuff and headed for the Homestead. The floodlights were out. By the time I had my skates laced on, my eyes were soaking up as much light as they could from the street. The practice backboard was a rectangular blot in the night. I slapped the puck with my stick. I couldn't see the puck sail into the darkness; I could only hear it knock against the backboard. This is what I do when things go wrong. (In the winter, anyway. I pull out hairs in the summer months.) I keep firing the puck into the board, letting it rebound to me. I stay directly in front of the backboard, and pretty close to it. That's to make sure I hit it. Because if I ever miss — well, the night is black and so's the puck — I know I'll never find it.

Megin

WHEN I WOKE UP, my cheek was resting on wood: my hockey stick. It's the thing I love most in the world, other than a few people. I got it one night when my father took Grosso and me to a Flyers game in the city. They were playing Wayne Gretzky and the Edmonton Oilers. Between periods the announcer called out a number; my father looked at my ticket stub and got all excited: "You won! You won!" What I won was a chance to go to the Oilers' locker room after the game and meet Wayne Gretzky. And as if that weren't enough, Wayne Gretzky gave me a hockey stick — a stick he himself had played with — and right then, he signed the handle: *"To Megin, from your friend Wayne Gretzky."* Grosso wanted to kill me, because he'd missed it by one number.

I kissed my stick and got up. It was the day after Christmas, first big day at Homestead Lake. A little while later, Sue Ann and I were standing on the shore. Most of the hockey players were already there, getting the kinks out. The nonhockey kids were at the other end, skating, falling, showing off their new clothes. Other kids were camped around the edges, scooping out snow — we call the scooped-out spots "nests" — laying down blankets, piling sticks for little fires. Some even had Sterno cans burning. I just let the whole scene soak in. I had my donuts, my cheese sandwiches, my thermos jug of hot chocolate, my hockey stuff, including my new Wayne Gretzky gloves.

I handed Sue Ann my food bag. "Here, make our place," I told her, and I pushed off onto the ice. Sue Ann loves making a nest more than skating. She always makes a big one and invites a lot of other girls over.

Valducci saw me coming. "Hey-hey —," he goes, "here she comes! Gretzky's little brother! Gretzky's little mother! Gretzky's lit —" That's as far as he got. My stick behind his skate, one quick yank, and Valducci's butt was on the ice.

After a while we chose up sides. As usual, Skelley and Broadhurst did the choosing. They're the two best players. As far back as I can remember, two things have always happened: (1) I get picked before El Grosso; (2) El Grosso gets mad. Sure enough, it happened again. I was Skelley's third pick. Grosso was Broadhurst's fifth. Oh yeah, another thing: we never get picked on the same team. They know better.

As usual, I called Sue Ann over to drop the puck for the opening face-off. As usual, she was terrified. She tiptoed on her skates across the ice to Skelley and Broadhurst, a mouse between two alley cats. She stayed as far away from them as she could, stretching her arms and body as far as possible to dangle the puck between them. She held it like something hot or dead, between the tips of two fingers. Then she dropped it and went screaming off the ice, holding her ears between her mittens.

At last: the first game of the season. Hah! The first game of the season was about two seconds old when I got slammed into and wound up butt-down on the ice. I looked up in time to see Grosso heading away. Didn't bother me. The day was long. Pretty soon I got my chance to retaliate. We were whipping the puck around Broadhurst's goal, looking for an opening. Skelley cruised behind the net, spotted me in front, fed me a pass, but Grosso got in the way and blocked it. That's when I made my move. Before Grosso could go anywhere with the puck, I body-checked him from behind. He went sprawling belly-down into the goal — a human puck! Meanwhile, the real puck was left sitting there at my feet. I wound up and fired a blur past Grosso's ear, under the goalie's armpit, smack into the upper right corner of the net. Score!

The whole Skelley team mobbed me. It was like what happens to Gretzky all the time. Then Grosso came charging, flailing his stick. "She fouled me! She hit me from behind!"

"You fouled me before," I shot back. "I just got you back, that's all."

Grosso stood there fuming, glaring. "Okay, girl, you asked for it."

"Anytime, chump."

Valducci started pounding the ice with his stick. "Yeah yeah! Let's have some action, baby! Ak-*shun!* Woogah!"

Sorry, Valducci, but your friend Grosso is too slow and clumsy to give me any action. Grosso can get from one point to another okay, and every once in a while (maybe twice a year) he scores a fluky goal, but when it comes to skating and to stick handling, he's not in my class. And he knows it. That's why he's always trying to body-check me to the other side of town. But as long as I keep one eye peeled for him, I'm okay. I see him charging, I step aside, and he goes crashing into the goal or the fence or somebody.

Hockeywise, the day just got better and better. We won our first game, 5 to 2. (First team with 5 points wins.) Then they picked sides again. This time I was Skelley's second pick. Broadhurst never picks me. He says he just doesn't want a girl on his team, but I think he's afraid of embarrassing Grosso by picking me over him. By midafternoon I was Skelley's number-one pick.

We won all our games except one. I was hot. I must have scored twenty goals that day. I even scored a hat trick — three goals in one game. My first hat trick ever! And the third goal happened to win that particular game, 5 to 4. My team went crazy. I felt myself being lifted; somebody was hauling me around the ice on his shoulders. It was John Poff. He's not much of a skater, but he sure gives a good ride around the ice. And a safe one — *nobody* body-checks Poff.

After every couple games I'd plop down in our nest and do a little eating. Sometimes I'd stick a donut in my pocket so I could grab some quick energy during the action. By the time the sun was setting and the floodlights came on, I was down to my last cheese sandwich and blueberry-filled. Nobody was in our nest, so I was munching away on the sandwich by myself when I heard some girls calling my name. They were waving, a bunch of them. I headed over, and the closer I got, the less I could believe my eyes. It was the biggest, most glorious nest I ever saw: *five* blankets (the biggest I ever saw before had two), a layback beach chair, a sofa, and Sterno cans warming two copper pots. In front of all this was a green, fake-grass mat saying WELCOME and, stuck in the snow, a five-foot-high plastic palm tree.

About twenty kids — nearly all the nonhockey seventh-graders — were there, most of them crowded around the Sterno fires. And who was lounging on the sofa? Who else — Zoe, all decked out in red and silver. She wore red earmuffs, with silver hoop earrings dangling from *them*. She was lying on her side, dipping little diamond-shaped crackers into a bowl of green stuff.

"What's that?" I asked her.

"Avocado dip."

I threw out my arms. "And what's all this?"

"Oh," she sighed, dipping, "just a little touch of home."

"Wha'd you do, have a moving truck?"

"Our station wagon."

"Yeah, but still —"

She reached behind the sofa, pulled something. I heard a hiss, then it stopped. "Inflatable," she said. She bounced up and over to the plastic palm tree. She flipped something on it — down came the green top, like an umbrella. "Collapsible."

"Are all you Californians like this?" I asked her.

"Only the goochies," she said. "Here, step into the dining room." She wedged into the crowd at the pots and came out with a long, skinny fork with a chunk of something gooey stuck on the end. She held it in front of my face. "Here, quick, before it drips." I opened my mouth, she shoved it in. It was soft, chewy, cheesy. "Fondue," she said.

I loved it. "Here, hold this." I handed her my sandwich, took the fork, and headed for the copper pots. I did like everybody else: stabbed a chunk of bread with the fork, dipped it in the melted cheese, ate.

By the time I turned away from the pots, I must have been fifty pounds heavier. I could hardly move. I was wondering where to put my used fork when I saw some sticking in the snow at the edge of the blankets. When I got closer, I saw the forks were also sticking into something that was lying on the snow. It was a photograph, in color — the kind they take at the mall, of little kids on Santa's lap. Only the kid on this Santa was a big kid. I couldn't tell who it was because a couple forks were stuck right in his face.

It was almost dark. This is always the neatest-looking time: the red strip of sky behind the Homestead House, the ice looking blue, the lights of little stick fires and Sterno cans and candles ringing the lake, skaters skating, nesters nesting. You can always tell the ninth-grade nests; they're the smallest; usually big enough for just two, barely.

"Megin! Look!"

It was Sue Ann. She was pointing across the ice, at our nest. Somebody — Grosso — was reaching down, rooting around, picking something up, sniffing it, skating away, dropping the something to the ice, pushing it with his stick ... *my blueberry-filled!*

By the time I got there he was passing the donut around with Valducci and Broadhurst and some of the other clowns. I chased it and tried to cut off the passes, but I was full of fondue and they were spread out too far. They were having a great old time, just standing there and passing the donut and howling with laughter. After a while I was just standing there in the middle, panting. Then Grosso cooed, "Okay, here ya go. You can have it back." He wound up and slap-shot the donut: blueberry glop.

Grosso knew better than to stick around. By the time I took off after him, he was halfway across the ice. Not that it did him any good; he's a turtle. A couple good strides and I was up to him. I took dead aim on his butt and swung my stick with both hands, baseball style. He yowled to the moon like a coyote.

Then I was the one being chased, which is a piece of cake for me. In fact, I turned around and skated backward, and still the turtle couldn't catch me. Every couple strides I'd flick my stick out and poke him in the stomach, and he'd grunt and fume and snort even more. "Me matador; you bull." The seventh-graders were cheering me on. I waved at them.

Then I decided to teach him a lesson. One of Grosso's many faults is that he can't stop good. I turned and took off fast. When I got near the edge of the lake, I pretended to slip and go out of control. While I was lurching around pretending to get my balance, I kept him in the corner of my eye. He was coming like a freight train, his stick back-swinging, then coming forward — I jammed my toe into the ice and shot to the side; I felt the breeze from his stick as he went by. He plowed into the snow and went flopping all over a pair of ninth-graders in their nest.

"Learn to stop, chump!" I called as I laughed and glided back to a hero's welcome at Zoe's palace.

Greg

THREE times I saw Sara Bellamy with Leo Borlock. Three thousand times I almost called Jennifer Wade on the phone. I never thought about calling Sara. But I did think about her. Sara never looked at me anymore, or spoke. It was like I was invisible to her. Of course, Jennifer Wade never saw me or spoke to me either. But would she, if we went to the same school? Or would I be invisible to her too?

When I tried to picture Jennifer real clear, I didn't have much to go on except the night at Sara's party. So I thought about that a lot, especially her touch on my arm. Only sometimes a funny thing happened. I would be picturing the fingers on my arm, and even feeling them, and I would look up and see Sara's face, not Jennifer's. When I thought of Sara, I usually pictured her with Leo, or her in her new powder blue scarf and cap. Only sometimes — crazy — it would be Jennifer's face in the scarf and cap. But it was never Jennifer with Leo.

I wondered what Sara and Leo talked about. Did they

talk about me a lot? What did she say when she first went to him? "Help me"? What would he say to me if I went to him? I tried to imagine:

ME. I have a problem.
LEO. Okay. What is it?
ME. Sara and Jennifer.
LEO. Right. Easy. One question: Who's the prettiest?
ME. Jennifer.
LEO. That's the answer. Go get her. Next patient.

Thinking about it that way, it seemed so simple. But it wasn't. And I couldn't really talk to Leo about it. There was nobody I could talk to about it. All I could do was wonder. I wondered and wondered and wondered.

I hadn't lifted a weight since Christmas. My vein was in hibernation.

The first time I saw Sara and Leo was at the mall, going into the bookstore.

The second time was at Homestead Lake on the day after Christmas. It was late afternoon when I noticed them nesting just off the edge of the ice. From then on, even though I was playing hockey, I was always aware of them. A couple times I snuck a look and saw them laughing. Were they laughing at me?

After dark, when the floodlights covered the ice, I got a closer look, a real close look. I was chasing down a loose puck to the lake's edge when my skate blade snagged in a rut and threw me right into their laps. For a split second, as I scrambled to my knees, Sara's face was right in front of mine. Her mouth and eyes were wide open — in shock, I guess — but it reminded me of a face singing Christmas carols. Her powder blue scarf, up close, had a fuzzy look to it, like cotton candy. It was piled high around her neck and covered her chin. Her cap was tilted on her head, like a beret. In that instant the thought came to me: she's cute.

I was cool. "Hey, fancy meeting you two here." I laughed, and was gone. As I skated back to the nets, I noticed I was a little shaky. And there was a taste in my mouth, from the words that had come out of it: "you two." The taste was bitter.

The third time I saw them together was the night of the school play. I don't really care that much about plays, but I figured I'd go to see if Valducci did anything crazy with the lights. I got there early, so I could go up to see Valducci. I asked him what special lighting effects he had in mind.

He shook his head. "None, baby. I'm goin' straight."

"Not with that California girl on stage, you're not."

"No, really." He patted his spotlight. "I'm in control. MacWilliams gave me the word."

"Yeah? Wha'd he say?"

"He said if I messed around, he'd have me arrested."

I laughed. "Executed too, huh?"

Valducci wasn't laughing. "No, listen, I think he meant it. Y'know how he yells? Hollers?"

"Yeah."

"Hollers the same thing over and over?"

"Yeah."

"He was different this time. He said it real quiet. And only once. That was it. Said it, left. Boom."

In a way, I was disappointed. Valducci comes in handy sometimes, because the things nobody else has the nerve to do, he does. It was strange seeing him so serious, so normal. "He's just trying to scare you," I said.

"He ain't tryin' — he's *doin'* it. And I ain't goin' to the slammer. No way, Joccalocca."

I went downstairs and took a seat in the back. When Sara went walking by with Leo Borlock, I knew Valducci wasn't the only reason I had shown up for the play. Again: the powder blue scarf and cap. And more this time. Earrings. And she was taller. High heels. She was dressed up! Down the aisle they went, following the usherette. The usherette stopped at a row about halfway down and handed each of them a program. The usherette nodded and smiled at them. They nodded and smiled at her. They went in to their seats. Before sitting down, he took his coat off — a long, man-type coat. She sat down and then pulled her scarf off. Then she plucked off her cap and gave her head a quick little shake. Then he tilted his head toward her and said something, and then he was putting his arm around her shoulders and holding her coat while she turned this way, that way, and slipped out of it. He let the coat fall over the back of her seat. About a minute later she tilted her head toward him, and then he was reaching around again and pulling the coat back up. It took him a long long time to get the coat just right on her shoulders.

I moved to a closer seat, on the other side of the aisle, about three rows behind them. Once, she looked around. I ducked and pretended to be tying my sneakers.

The worst thing about the play starting was that the lights in the audience went out. I panicked. I wanted to move right behind them, but by then every seat was taken.

The play was a hit from the start. The audience was almost always either clapping or laughing. Romeo, who is really Jeremy Bach, got laughs from the parents because they thought he was funny, and from the students because he's such an egotistical pretty boy. He thinks he really is

141

Romeo. As for the Zoe girl from California, I had to admit she was pretty good. You'd never guess she was only a seventh-grader, especially not in the micro-mini McDonald's outfit she was wearing.

Valducci stayed in control, like he said. When Romeo and Juliet first met at the Dipsy Dumpster and sang to each other and had their first kiss, the stage was dark except for the spotlight, and the spotlight never wavered. As far as I could tell, all through the first act, Valducci was in control.

That's more than I could say for me. The cozier Romeo and Juliet got up on the stage, the itchier I got. I couldn't help thinking: Romeo and Juliet equals Leo and Sara. When the lights blazed on at the end of Act One, I almost had a stroke; they were getting up! They were leaving their seats, edging out to the aisle, walking to the back. *Oh no! They're going somewhere to make out!* I followed them out to the lobby. They stood and talked with some other kids. Sara laughed a lot. I didn't remember her laughing so much when she was with me. Then they headed down a hallway. *Oh no!* But they stopped and looked at a case displaying stuff from art classes. The ceiling lights flickered. The people started heading for their seats. I hung back, to make sure they went along with the crowd. They did. Two whole acts to go. I wasn't sure I could make it.

Act Two was worse. Romeo and Juliet getting cozier and cozier. I must have ruptured my eyeballs trying to spot Sara and Leo in all the clumpy darkness. At the funny parts I swore I could pick out her laughter from all the others. Such a great time she was having. Was Leo fixing her coat over her shoulder? Did he stop playing games by now and just flat-out put his arm around her? Were they holding hands, secretly, on the armrest between them? On his side? On her side? Fingers intertwined? Onstage, things were all of a sudden going bad for Romeo and Juliet. Their parents were tearing them apart, Romeo banished to a natural foods shop, Juliet to a White Tower. *Great*, I thought. But then they escaped and met again, at the usual place. She climbed into the Dumpster with him and Act Two ended as the lid slowly lowered to a soft clank and the stage became dark and silent.

I was into the lobby before the lights went on. I tore up the stairs, into the lighting room, shocking Valducci. "I'm going crazy!" I blurted.

He grinned. "Join the club."

At that moment I felt a bond with Valducci. His Zoe, my Sara. And both of us on the outside. Then he said something that floored me. "Sara Bellamy, right?"

"How'd you know?" I said after I recovered.

"The way she was all over you on the sled that day. Her chasing you into the woods."

"We didn't do anything."

" 'Course not."

"No kidding. She never caught me."

"What?"

"She didn't catch me."

"You mean you really *were* running away? You didn't *let* her catch you?"

"No."

He put his hand on my forehead. "This boy's sick. He runs *away* from girls."

"Not anymore."

"But now," he grinned, "she's here with Leo the Shrink."

"You saw them?"

He tapped on his window. "I see everything."

"I wish I could. I'm going crazy wondering what they're doing there in the dark."

"Maybe they're watching the play."

"Yeah, well, what if it was you and Zoe sitting there? What would you be doing?"

He whistled and fanned his face. "Makes me get all overheated just thinking about it. You're right, you got a problem."

"Thanks a lot, pal." I started to go.

"Yo — Greg —," he called. "Hey, you like this chick, huh?"

With all my scrambled feelings lately, the idea had never occurred to me that way: so simple, so blunt. "Yeah" — I shrugged — "yeah." And then it all came gushing out. I told him about Jennifer Wade and lifting weights all summer and getting stopped by the cop and Sara's party and the bracelet and the good letter and the bad phone call and Sara and Leo —

Music below — Valducci jumped. "It's starting!" He whirled and started flipping switches and running his finger down the script. I left him there, hunched over the controls, mumbling to himself.

I walked the hallways. Cold green cinderblock walls. Cold gray linoleum. Sounds from the auditorium came in quick, faint bursts — a brassy blare, a shriek of human voices — like a faraway radio that was trying to die. So easy, I thought, so easy to walk away from the world. The stairwells, nothing reached there.

Then, somewhere, somewhere behind me — not far, not the auditorium: a noise, two noises. A squeal (girl-type), then a door-slam. *Them!* I turned, went back down the hallway. Door by door, telling nothing, dark. I was tiptoe-ing, I stopped, listened: nothing. Where? Which door? That one? 206? 208? 210? My heart stopped: Faculty Lounge! Sofas inside. Rugs. I stood at the door, sweating, my hand trembling on the knob. I thought of the time I french-kissed her, her head bumping against the door, the little yelp. *No, Borlock, you can't!* I threw the door open, fumbled for the light switch, flipped it on: empty. Chairs, magazines, coffee maker, deck of cards. No sofa.

I headed back for the play, not sure what I'd proved. That they weren't in the Faculty Lounge? Or that I'd opened the wrong door?

The finale was on. I stood in back. Romeo and Juliet were married under the golden arches. Then, while all the counter girls and busboys and customers and even parents cheered and danced around, the happy couple climbed into their honeymoon special — a McWhopper — and they wrapped their arms around each other and sang "Ham-burger Built for Two," and then while everybody did the Burger Boogie around the newlyweds and showered them with french fries, they laid a titanic kiss on each other. Meanwhile the lights went absolutely crazy wild bananas. Flashing, swooping, slashing everywhere — walls, ceiling, audience — like being inside a tornado of lights. Poor Val-ducci, he couldn't quite hold out long enough. Would he really be arrested?

Then I noticed people in the audience laughing — at the lights. Some even turned around and looked up at the con-trol room and applauded. I guess they figured it was all part of the finale. Then I saw something that gave me the chills. In the center of all the crazy, swirling lights, a single beam — the spotlight — never even moved, not an inch. It shone straight down, smack into the middle of the audience, silent and frosty and still, and nobody was noticing it—nobody but me.

I started down the aisle. I kept moving until I could see what I already knew—that the light was landing on Sara Bellamy and Leo Borlock. They were here, thank God, here, not upstairs! They were *not* snuggled up to each other. His arm was *not* around her. I wanted to laugh, I wanted to cry, I wanted to hug somebody. The people were standing now, clapping, whistling. I turned and looked up to the point where the shaft of light began and I saluted my friend, Edward P. Valducci.

The next morning, Saturday, I phoned my Health teacher, Mrs. Ackerman, at her home.

" 'Lo?" She sounded a little groggy.

"Hello? Mrs. Ackerman?"

"Mm."

"This is Greg Tofer. In your Health class? Ninth grade?"

"Mm."

"Uh, Mrs. Ackerman, you know the egg project? Y'know?"

"Is this 'bout school?"

"Yes, the egg project. Remember, you asked for people to volunteer as couples? Like parents for the egg?" Silence. "Well, I just thought you'd like to know that Sara Bellamy and I would like to be a pair. Of parents. For the egg. Okay?" Silence. "Mrs. Ackerman?"

"Isn't this Saturday?"

"That's right. Okay, Mrs. Ackerman? Greg Tofer. Sara Bellamy. Tofer. Bellamy. Egg project. Okay?" The phone went click. I grinned to myself. "Okay."

Megin

ONE GOOD THING about having a birthday on January 30: it's like getting a second shot at Christmas.

When I stopped at Emilie's after school, she handed me a box wrapped in beautiful paper and ribbons. "Don't open it till you get home," she said.

"Why not?"

"Oh, it's not anything I knitted or cookies I baked or preserves that I preserved. Nothing grandmotherly."

"Bull," I said. I tore the paper off. The box was from Beck's, a high-class department store. What could it be? I opened it: donuts. A dozen — blueberry-filled, every one.

"I know they're your favorites," she said. "I thought I'd fool you with the box."

I hugged her. "Thank you," I whispered into her white hair, "thank you, thank you . . . Grandmom."

I felt her flinch. "I can't knit."

I buttoned her lips with my finger. I kissed her on the nose. "Grrrr-randmom."

* * *

Instead of a party ("You had parties the last two years," my mother whined), I was allowed to have two friends overnight. I asked Sue Ann, of course — and Zoe.

"Zoe?" Sue Ann gasped when I told her. "Zoe *Miranda?*"

"No, dummy, Zoe Murphy."

"Eeek."

"Sue Ann, you're the one that was always telling me all about her. What're you afraid of?"

"I never thought I'd be *sleeping* with her."

I cracked up. I slapped her on the back. "Don't worry, I'll protect you. You sleep with your monkey, I'll sleep with Zoe."

In the kitchen that night, as I was helping get the refreshments ready, my mother whispered, "A little on the flashy side, isn't she?"

"Who?" I said, as if I didn't know.

"Your friend. Flo?"

"Zoe, Mom."

"Zoe."

I whispered in her ear. "She's from California."

Her eyebrows went up, she nodded — "Oh" — and went on scooping ice cream.

Then my father came in. "Your, uh, friend — Bo?"

"Zoe."

"Zoe. Didn't you say she's in seventh grade?"

"She is."

He was staring at my face, but I knew where his thinking was: How can two bodies so different both be in seventh grade? He said, "What happened? Was she left back a couple of years?" I kicked him in the shin. He ouched.

148

My mother whispered, "She's from California." He limped out of the kitchen.

When the candles on the cake were lit, I went into my huff. (Never have I not gotten every candle on the first blow.) "Hold it!" my father said. "We're not all here."

I looked around the table. "We are so."

"Greg's not here."

"Who's Greg?" asked Zoe.

"The family animal," I said.

"Greg is Megin's brother," my mother butted in.

"I'm Megin's brudder!" wailed Toddie. "Greg is a animal!" He was standing on his chair next to Zoe. He had one arm around her, and with the finger of his other hand he was tracing circles inside the hoop of her earring. Toddie and Zoe had fallen in love at first sight, and they were already planning to get married.

Zoe kissed him. "Don't worry, Toddsie, he could never take me away from you. You're too much of a man."

Toddie swelled up like a balloon. I prayed he wouldn't fart.

My father went to the foot of the stairs. "Greg, come on! We're having the cake now!"

Grosso's voice came down. "I'm in the bathroom. Go ahead without me."

"Hurry up! We'll wait!" my father called.

"Daddy," I groaned, "come *on*. Who cares? You know he's just stalling. He doesn't want to be here."

"Of course he wants to be here."

Barf. My father and his happy-little-family routine. *Everybody* has to be around the table for *every* birthday. "Daddy," I said, "what's the point? He's not gonna sing anyway." Grosso and I never sing at each other's birthdays. My father didn't answer; he just waited. Finally the toilet flushed upstairs, and about a year later Grosso showed up. Toddie hugged Zoe with both arms and scowled across the table. "Mine," he said.

"You're right, Toddsie," whispered Zoe, "he *is* an animal."

My mother scowled at Zoe.

So everybody sang — every *human being*, that is — and I blew out the candles on the first try, all thirteen of them, plus the one to grow on.

Most of the presents I got were nice, but sort of ordinary. I saved Zoe's till last; I expected something pretty goochy. It was something to wear — silky, turquoise background with lots of little curlicues and big butterflies. Reminded me of wallpaper. I took it out of the box, held it up. "A robe."

Zoe sighed. "It's a kimono."

"Ouuu, very nice," cooed my mother.

"Stunning," piped my father. "Come on, Dimpus, try it on."

I put it on. "Ah, gee, Zoe, it's a little big."

My parents and Zoe laughed. "You wrap it around," said Zoe. "Wrap it around."

I guess I didn't wrap it around right, because pretty soon Zoe was standing behind me, reaching around and doing the wrapping. I felt like a mummy. I was beginning to wish she had gotten me a nice ordinary pair of sweat socks. Sue Ann was snickering. I grabbed Zoe's hands, unwrapped myself, and shoved the kimono at her. "Here, Zoe, *you* put it on. *You* model it."

Well, that was like telling Bugs Bunny to eat a carrot. Zoe carried the kimono out through the living room and partway up the stairway, where we couldn't see her. When she reappeared, coming out of the darkness into the light of the chandelier, she was the most gorgeous person I ever saw. The kimono came down to her feet, which were bare. Her turquoise toenails matched the kimono perfectly. And the way she moved — not regular walking — I guess it's what slinking is. Toddie was all boggles, like he was seeing Santa Claus. In fact, everybody was boggles. Dead, boggled silence, except for some faint, gulpy sort of noises that I think were coming from my father.

The doorbell rang, startling everybody. Grosso answered it. "Oh no," I heard Zoe say. It was Valducci. Grosso led him upstairs, but not before Valducci crashed into the coffee table and tripped over the first step, gawking at Zoe.

"What's *he* doing here?" I demanded.

"He's staying over with Greg," my mother said.

"Mom! The only reason Grosso asked him over" — I looked at Zoe, who was taking off the kimono, "— ah, never mind. I thought this was supposed to be *my* birthday. *My* friends."

She got up and started clearing the table. "Don't worry. They won't bother you."

Right, Mom. As soon as we headed upstairs, the trouble started. "Uh-oh," went Zoe. She had left two silver boots on the steps. Only one was there now.

I was in Grosso's room in a microsecond. "Okay, where is it?"

"Get outta here," snarled Grosso. "This is my room."

"Where is it?"

"Where's what?"

"The boot."

"Boot?" Grosso and Valducci looked at each other like I was speaking Greek. "What boot?"

151

I started yanking drawers open. He slammed one shut, almost decapitating my fingers. Then, from behind me: "Val-dooooo-cci. Where's my boooo-ty?" Zoe was purring against the doorway, fluttering her turquoise fingernails into the room. Valducci, like he was hypnotized, reached under the bed, brought out the boot, and handed it to her.

"Ninth-grade punks," I said as we turned and went out.

When Zoe got to my room she screamed. I rushed in. "What's the matter?"

"Look!"

"Look at what?"

"Your *room!*"

Sue Ann was giggling. I kicked her. "Doggone that Toddie," I said. "He musta been in my room again. He's always slopping up the place." I used my hockey stick to sweep a path across the room. "Madam" — I bowed — "your bed."

As soon as we were settled into my room, I phoned for a pizza (part of my birthday present from my parents). I ordered a large. One-third pepperoni (me), one-third extra cheese (Sue Ann), and one-third anchovies (Zoe, ugh!). About a half-hour later, we were deep into a game of poker (Zoe was teaching us) when there came a knock on my door. "What is it?" I called.

"Pizza," said a voice. Sounded Italian.

I jumped up, opened the door. It was Valducci, holding a pizza box. "Itsa you pizza, ma'am. Somma pepparone, somma extra cheesa, somma anchovy. Eh, who wantsa de anchovy?" His eyeballs were crawling over my shoulder and into the room. I grabbed the box and shut the door.

That's kind of how things went. We would be doing stuff, and one way or another we kept getting interrupted. Once, a piece of paper came sliding under the door. It was a letter from a talent scout looking for a female lead for a movie version of *Romeo and Juliet*. Other times Toddie was sent in with weird messages. Other times there were strange noises outside the door. Once there was a strange smell. There were also tapping noises on the windows. One time Sue Ann went to the back window and screeched. We rushed over. Down in the backyard, in the dim light from the kitchen window, I could make out a person, a body, sprawled facedown, with something — a tomato plant stake — sticking out of his back. I just shook my head and pulled down the shade. "Gotta hand it to him. Almost looks real."

"What's the *matter* with him?" said Zoe.

I figured it was time to start dishing it out. And what I had in mind was some real pain. I waited till the "dead body" had time to get up and come back upstairs. I knew they would be in Grosso's room watching TV, probably with the door open. I handed Zoe the kimono and told her to put it on. "Now," I said, "I want you to go slinking down the hall to the bathroom. Slow."

Her eyes lit up. "Past *their* room?"

"You got it." She started off. I whispered after her: "*Slink!*"

Boy, did she slink. Must have taken her ten minutes just to go from one side of their doorway to the other. She stayed in the bathroom a minute, then slunk back. As soon as she passed their room, an eyeball popped out of the doorway.

"Go back," I told her when she got up to us. "We're gonna kill him."

She took off again, down the hallway, back. This time, besides the eyeball, there were noises — scratchy, squeaky noises — coming from the doorway. I shoved her out again.

153

"Go, girl, slink. Die, Valducci." This time Zoe even out-slunk herself. She *oozed*. As she went past the doorway, a hand came out, clawing the air after her.

Four more times I sent Zoe down the hallway. After the fourth time, we stood there, listening. If I didn't know better, I would have sworn there was a cage down there with a hungry, hyper, constipated chimpanzee trying to get out. Zoe looked at me. "Enough?"

I nodded. "Enough." We slapped hands and closed the door.

The rest of the night was ours: cold pizza, TV, poker, talking, laughing. Only once more did a knock come at the door. My mother: "Okay, girls, you can stay up as late as you want, but try to keep the noise down. Better get your pj's on."

Sue Ann and I looked at each other: *Uh-oh*. Usually when Sue Ann stays over, we take turns going into my closet to get changed. But now, with Zoe Miranda in the room, things were different. I wasn't sure how, just different.

Well, while Sue Ann and I were there gaping at each other, Zoe strolled over to the bed and started taking things off — like there was nobody around! I stopped breathing. Off and off the clothes kept coming, till there was nothing left except two hoop earrings and twenty turquoise toe- and fingernails. Then she sat on the bed, hoisted one foot up, examined it, reached into her travel bag, fished out a nail file, and proceeded to file away at her big toenail. Then she did the other big toe. Then she stood up, full-front to us, more naked body than I ever saw except for Toddie as a baby, and she started across the room, *toward Sue Ann*. Instantly two things happened: Sue Ann grabbed her monkey, and I flicked off the bedroom light.

As it turned out, Zoe was heading for the picture of Emilie. "Hey," she growled, "leave the light on. I can't see this."

"We can see the TV better this way," I said.

"Megin! Turn it on!"

I turned it on. Sue Ann was now in the farthest corner of the room.

"Who is this, anyway?" said Zoe.

"Oh, just some friend of mine." I turned off the light.

"Megin!" I turned it on. "Hey, is this —?" *Uh-oh.* Now she was coming over to *me.* I couldn't think. How can you think when there's a stark-naked Californian standing right next to you? "Is the rabbit real?" she said.

"Uh, yeah, real."

"Weird," she muttered and put the picture back. I turned off the light.

Zoe, like nothing had ever happened, went back to her bag and put her pj's on — if you can call baby-dolls pj's. Sue Ann and I went to work in opposite dark corners and finally got ours on too.

The sleeping arrangements were: me and Zoe on the bed, Sue Ann on blankets on the floor. Zoe offered to trade with Sue Ann. "No, you stay," I told her. "First-time visitors always get the bed. And the window side." Then she suggested that Sue Ann climb in with us, since I have a big double bed. "Wouldn't work," I said. "The monkey can't stand heights." We all laughed, Sue Ann hysterically.

We settled into watching TV. First a rerun of *Saturday Night Live.* Then a movie about giant worms taking over the earth. By the time the worms were crawling up the dome of the Capitol in Washington, D.C., I was pretty zonked out. " 'Night," I said.

" 'Night," said Zoe. " 'Night, Sue Ann."

Sue Ann didn't answer her, not right then anyway—not till a couple minutes went by: " 'Night, Zoe."

"Wow," said Zoe, "that's what I call a delayed reaction."

I didn't say anything, but I knew why Sue Ann hadn't answered right away: she'd been saying her prayers. She always does. Which reminded me to say mine before I conked out completely.

When I opened my eyes again, Zoe was still sitting up, but she wasn't facing the TV. She was holding the shade aside and looking out the window, toward the sky. I was going to say something to her. I was going to ask her if she missed California. But then I figured I'd better not, because she might be saying *her* prayers, to Halley's comet. I could see twinkling stars framed in the hoop of one of her earrings.

Greg

I COULD HAVE SKATED on the look Sara was giving me from across the room. Mrs. Ackerman had just read off the list of egg couples, ending with: "Tofer-Bellamy."

There were thirteen shoe boxes on Mrs. Ackerman's desk. She put one egg in each of them. Then she called us up and gave a box to each couple. She came around in front of her desk, smiled. "Congratulations. Each of you is the proud parent of a healthy new baby. I don't have any speeches to make now. We'll let the experience speak for itself." Then she gave us the rules:

1. For the next seven days we would never call the egg an egg. It was a baby.
2. We would never let the baby out of our sight, and would always keep it close enough to be able to hear it cry.
3. Mother and father would alternate taking the baby home overnight. Fathers would have the first night.
4. Decide what sex your baby is, and give it a name.

She said our grades will depend on two things: (1) if the baby makes it through the week; (2) a report each couple will have to write. If your baby doesn't make it through the week, the highest grade you can get is a C. And no sneaking in a substitute for a broken egg — each egg has a special mark.

Then she asked for questions. One boy — father — asked why the babies were in shoe boxes. Couldn't they be in something more convenient? "Who says babies are convenient?" she said. A mother asked, giggling, if she could do something to make her baby more comfortable in its box. "It's *your* baby," smiled Mrs. Ackerman.

When class was over, Sara handed the baby to me and took off. I went after her. "Hey, how about that? We wound up as a couple."

"Amazing coincidence."

"You're not mad, are you?"

"No, I'm overjoyed. Can't you tell?"

"Well, what's it gonna be?"

"What are you talking about?"

"Boy or girl?"

"I don't care."

"You don't care? You're the mother."

"Don't remind me. Pick whatever you want." She went into her English class.

"How about a girl?" I called.

She returned to the doorway long enough to sneer, "Fine. Then you can name it Jennifer."

Well, I didn't exactly feel like a proud papa the rest of the day. At lunch most of the other couples sat together, their shoe boxes on their tables. They seemed to be enjoying it, really getting into it. Families.

After school, when the fathers took the babies home with them on buses, the mothers waved from the the sidewalk.

"New sneakers?" my mother said when I got home. (My shoe box said NIKE on it.)

"No," I said, "it's not sneakers." I knew she wouldn't ask me any more about it, so I told her. "It's a school project for Health. We all got eggs" — I showed her the egg, "— one egg for each couple. It's supposed to be a baby."

She winced. "A *what?*"

"Baby. We gotta pretend it's a baby."

"Why?"

"I don't know. The experience is supposed to speak to us."

"Well," she said, heading off, "that baby better not speak to me. I've had enough babies speak to me."

Boy or girl? That wasn't hard. I knew I wanted it to be a girl. But what to name it? Sara? No, shouldn't be the same as her. But something to do with her. Something she would like. It came to me: something French. I got the dictionary, turned to the back, where it said "Names of Women." I went down the list, stopping at the names with "Fr." after them, until I came to the right one.

"Camille," I said as I came up behind Sara at her locker next morning.

She didn't bother to turn. "What?"

"Camille. How's that for a name?"

"Fine." She got her books, smacked her locker shut, and for the first time looked at the shoe box. She snarled. "Oh great."

"What's the matter?"

"Look at the others. You'll see what the matter is." She grabbed the box and stomped off to her homeroom.

Pretty soon I saw what she meant. The others' shoe boxes, well, they no longer looked like shoe boxes. They were decorated — some with paper, some with paint, usually pink or blue. And there were little blankets inside, and little pillows. I felt bad, thinking of Sara carrying around a bare box. No wonder she was mad. She was looking like a bad mother. "Hey, Tofe," one of the fathers called in the hall, "I see you named your kid Nike. That a boy or girl?"

One of the mothers said to me, "Sara's motherly instincts are being violated." She was grinning, but I don't think she was joking.

I caught Sara coming out of French. I told her I was sorry I hadn't fixed up the box, and sorry that her motherly instincts were being violated.

"Who cares about motherly instincts?" she snapped. "I just want a good grade." She ducked into a girls' room.

When I saw her after lunch I said, "Y'know, if you'd talk to me maybe things would be better. The other mothers talk to the fathers. We're supposed to do what's best for the baby."

"It is not a baby," she seethed, "it is an egg."

After school, at her locker: "Sara?"

She sighed. "What now?"

"A lot of the parents are getting together tonight —"

She stomped her foot. "Stop saying that! We are not parents!" She bashed her locker door shut and took off.

The box was still on the floor. I picked it up. "Sara — you forgot something."

She screeched, whirled, stomped back, snatched it out of my hands, and took off again. I could hear the egg rolling and knocking in the box. I went after her. I grabbed her arm and led her through a door and down some stairs. I was surprised she didn't fight back. On the landing half-way down she pulled out of my grasp. Her cheeks were red. She was glaring at me, hating me, breathing hard. Suddenly my head was out of words, and reasons for being there. What finally came out was: "I like that new scarf and hat you got. The powder blue."

"What do you want?" Her eyes were glistening.

"Sara . . . look . . . I'm sorry."

She snickered. "Is that why you dragged me down here? Don't worry about it. *I'll* fix up the box." She started up the stairs. I pulled her back down.

"That's not what I'm saying. That's not what I'm sorry for."

"Oh, I thought it was."

"Well yeah, yeah, I *am* sorry for that. But that's not the only thing."

"So what else is there?"

"Well . . . you know —"

"No, I don't know."

"Well . . . Jennifer."

"Jennifer? Jennifer who?"

"Come on, Sara."

Her glare was fierce. "Jennifer *who?*"

Just then some ninth-graders came stampeding down the stairs. We froze while they passed.

"Wade," I said. "C'mon now. Stop acting like you're not mad."

"You want me to act like I *am* mad?"

"No no, c'mon, you know what I mean."

"No," she said, "I don't know what you mean." She started up the stairs. I held her by the arm. She sighed into the space above my head. "I think I'm getting tired of this game."

"Sara, I *know* you're mad."

"What, pray tell, am I supposed to be mad at?"

"Me."

"*You?*"

"You hate me. I can see it. You can't stand me. You despise me."

She laughed. "De*spise* you? I don't even think about you, so how can I de*spise* you?"

She wrenched free. This time I didn't reach for her — not with hands anyway. "You *asked* me to kiss you," I called.

She was at the top step when she ran into the words, like they were a brick wall. She turned, real slow, looked down. "What did you say?"

"That time at your house, after the fair, remember? You said, 'Uh, you wouldn't need a ticket to kiss me.' Remember? And the time we were sledding. That's all I'm saying. That's what I've been *trying* to say. I know you're mad at me, and I can understand why, but what I'm saying is, I don't think you really have a right to be mad at me, because, like I said, you asked *me* to kiss *you.*" She was moving down the stairs. "And, like, *you* asked *me* to go to the Conestoga fair. And *you* asked *me* to your birthday party. That's all I'm saying. That's all."

By now she was on the step above me. She glared down for a long time. Little parts of her neck were the only things moving. Then she said, slow and cold, "You could have said no."

"What did you want," I said, "me to say no or to kiss you?"

She slapped me. I didn't even see it coming. I knew it

was hard, by the way her face shot out of my vision, but my skin didn't feel it. Then suddenly, a rolling sound — egg on cardboard — she was losing her balance, lurching forward, tripping down into me, the shoe box rattling along the stair posts, tilting, tilting, the egg rolling to the lip, over the edge, she screaming ... I caught it, before it hit the step. Smooth, gleaming, cool — so perfect — in my hand. Saved. For a long time there was only our breathing in the stillness. I put the egg, carefully, into a corner of the box. I wanted to look up, to her face, but I was afraid of what I'd find. I saw only the box rise in her hand, and then she was moving, running, down the stairs and out the door.

When Sara handed me the box next day, it was decorated: pink-and-white wrapping paper on the outside, and on the inside a little white mattress and pillow and a pink blanket. The blanket came up to the baby's chin.

"That's great," I said.

"I want an A," she said.

Okay, I was thinking that night, you want an A, I'll get you an A. I found some lace and pasted it around the edges of the box. I reinforced the inside of the box and then made two plywood half-moon rockers for the bottom. I made a hood for the top to keep the sun out of Camille's eyes. And finally I got from my mother an old baby rattle of mine and laid it on the blanket.

My mother was looking more and more suspicious. "You sure this is for Health class?" she said. "Or am I going to be a grandmother soon?"

I laughed.

I didn't say anything when I gave Sara the box next morning. Her eyes snapped open when she saw what I had done, but she didn't say anything either.

Later that morning I heard that one of the couples, Jeff Peterson and Ashley Vote, had lost their baby. Cracked on Jeff's kitchen floor. Rolled off the kitchen table as he was working on the box. "Ashley's crushed," a mother told me. Ashley looked it, when I saw her at lunch: red eyes, feebly poking at some Jell-O cubes, surrounded by girls trying to console her.

Next day, Friday, I took the box from Sara again without a word. It wasn't till third period that I noticed only the very tip of the egg was showing. I pulled the cover down, and that's when I saw the little pink pajamas, with feet, and the name *Camille* stitched in purple thread.

I felt great, super. I sailed through the rest of the day. I was tempted to try talking to Sara, but I figured now that she was starting to thaw out, I'd better not press my luck. Besides, I was still trying to work up the nerve to ask her to keep the baby on Sunday, which was supposed to be my day. Sunday was going to be the big hockey game: us Homestead House players against the Rink Rats from the Skatium. Hanging around the lake could be dangerous for a baby, egg or not. I was sure now that Sara would be willing to baby-sit an extra day, if only I could make myself ask her. I wished by some miracle she would call me and take the pressure off.

The miracle happened. About noon Saturday. When I heard her voice, I tried not to sound too thrilled.

"Hello? Greg?"

"Yeah?"

"This is Sara Bellamy."

"I know. Hi."

"Have a question to ask. Well, favor, sort of."

"Yeah. Sure."

"About the, uh, project. Would you mind keeping it today?"

"You mean the baby? The egg?"

"Yes. Will you?"

"Well, if you want, I guess."

"Thanks, bye—"

"Sara."

"What?"

"Hey, uh, by today, does that mean tonight too?"

A short pause. "Uh-huh. Okay?"

"I guess."

"Bye." She hung up.

Only then did my brain start working. In a couple seconds I was calling her back.

"Sara?"

"Yes?"

"This is Greg again."

Pause. "Yes?"

"I was just wondering, how come you can't take the baby today?"

"Well, I'll be busy."

"Busy tonight?"

"Yeah, sort of."

"Like on a date with somebody? Like with Leo Borlock?"

Long pause. "Is that any of your business?"

"Yeah, maybe it is, since you're asking me the big favor." Silence. "Well?"

"Well what?"

"You going out tonight?"

"What if I am?"

"And you don't want to be dragging a baby along, right?

165

You don't want it to get in the way between you and Leo, right?" Silence. "Right, Sara?" More silence. "Well, I got news for you. I'm bringing the baby over to your house. Right now. It's your job. You're the mother." She hung up.

I took the box to her house and left it on the porch.

It was a long Saturday night for me, thinking about Sara and Leo. Together. Somewhere. At first I was glad I made her take the baby. Keep them from concentrating too much on each other. But then I wasn't so sure. Didn't I hear somewhere that babies bring people closer together? A long, long Saturday night.

Next day, when I left the house for the big game, I found the baby back on my porch.

Megin

MY MOTHER'S WORDS stabbed me like an icicle to the heart: "Megin, I want you to take Toddie to the library tonight."

"Library?" I said. "He can't even read."

"Children's Story Hour. Puppets too."

"Can't Greg take him?"

"Greg took him last month."

"Can't Daddy take him?"

"Saturday night. He's working."

"Can I just leave him there and come right back?"

"Take him, stay there with him, and bring him back. Alive."

I took a deep breath and asked the big question: "What time?"

"Seven o'clock."

Arrrrgggh! I wanted to scream "No! Never!" and throw things through windows. But I didn't. I controlled myself. Remember Zoe, I told myself — how good an actress she is. Be an actress. Act.

So I acted. I nodded and said, "Okay, no problem." I even smiled a little. I got up from the dinner table and strolled away, all calm and cool. I didn't say a word about the Wayne Gretzky special on TV that night. At seven o'clock. I didn't say they were going to be talking with him and showing highlights of his best games, his most fantastic shots. I didn't tell my mother that nothing — not a flood coming down the street or the earth colliding with another planet or the Children's Story Hour — was going to keep me from being in front of my TV set at seven o'clock.

I had to work fast. It was already after six. By six-thirty I was ready. I left my bedroom door open, so my mother could hear. She was coming up the stairs, heading for my room, just steps away — *now, girl, act!* I toppled off my bed, hard, onto the floor: *thump.*

First I heard my mother's voice in the hallway: "What was that?" Then she was in my room. "Megin! What are you doing?"

"Nothin', Mom. I'm okay." I made my voice sound grunty but friendly.

"What did you do? Slip on an old pizza crust?"

I chuckled painfully. "Maybe it's an attack of cleano-phobia."

"Well," she said, "if it is, you better get over it pretty soon. It's almost time to go."

"I will, Mom. Don't worry."

"To tell you the truth, Megin, I wasn't all that worried. I just want you on your feet and ready to go."

"Right," I grunted. I reached up for her arm, clawed up to her shoulder, and pulled myself up. I put all my weight on her, so she was practically on her knees by the time I was standing.

She started to walk away. I collapsed to my knees. She turned. "Megin! *What* is going on?"

"Nothing, Mom," I answered cheerfully, clutching my stomach. "I'm okay. I'm ready to go. Is Toddie ready?"

"Megin, stand."

She took a quick step backward, so this time I had to pull myself up with my dresser. "There," I said, smiling, panting, "okay?"

She looked suspicious. "What's the problem?"

"Nothing, Mom, really. Just a little cramp, that's all."

"Cramp? Where?"

"I don't know. Around here." I pointed to a place.

"Maybe just a bad enough cramp to keep you from taking your little brother to the library, huh?" She was looking *very* suspicious.

I straightened up. "Mom, honest, look. I'm okay. I *want* to go. Really. C'mon now." I pushed her ahead of me into the hallway. "Let's go down. I gotta get my coat."

The next time I heard my mother's voice, I was in the living room ready to leave with Toddie. I had his hand. She howled from the kitchen. "Megin!"

"What, Mom?"

"What in *God's* name are you *doing?*"

"Goin' to the library, Mom."

"Crawling?" She'd noticed that I was down on all fours. "Are you planning on crawwwling all the way to the library?"

"Mom, it's okay. It feels better this way, that's all. No big deal."

Five minutes later I was in my bed (Mother's orders), under the covers with my Gretzky stick, watching TV and listening to Grosso squawking downstairs: "Mom, I'm telling ya, she's lying! She's faking it! She just doesn't wanna take him! I took him last month!"

Gretzky was great. He was great just sitting there talking in the studio, great being mobbed in the shopping malls, great waving in the parades. But most of all he was great on ice, weaving through the Black Hawk defense, beating the Canucks single-handed, hat-tricking the Maple Leafs. Gretzky was making mincemeat of the Jersey Devils when suddenly my bedroom light blazed on and my father came rushing in. He knelt by the bed, right in front of me, so I had to crane my neck to see Gretzky mopping up the Devils. He put his hand on my forehead. "Yep," he said, "you do seem a little warm."

I pushed his hand away. "Daddy, I'm *watching*." He turned off the TV. "Dad-deeee!"

"Calm down, Dimpus, easy, easy, no getting excited." He was petting me like a dog. "You dressed?" He pulled down my covers. "What's this?"

"My hockey stick."

"Oh — okay. Now, think you can stand up?"

For the first time I took a good look at him. His hair was messed up. He still had his coat on. He was breathing hard, like he was excited, or upset. Something dawned on me. "Hey — aren't you supposed to be working tonight?"

"I was. Mommy called me."

"Called? What for?" As soon as I asked the question, the answer hit me. "Daddy, did she tell you I was sick? I'm okay now. I just had a little cramp, that's all. Look—" I hopped out of bed, flicked the TV on, and started doing jumping jacks. My father tackled me, gently, turned off the TV, and dumped me back on the bed. He pinned me down with his hand. "Don't — move."

170

"Daddy, I'm okay."

"You can't be okay. Not from what I heard. And you know Mommy — she wouldn't call me unless it was serious."

He was right about that. I must have done a great job of acting. "Yeah, but Dad, it feels a lot better now. Especially since I was watching TV. It was distracting me. Can I put it back on?"

He wasn't even listening. He was just giving me this silly grin and wagging his head and looking really goofy. Suddenly he was hugging me and mumbling into my hair. "I'm really proud of you, you little trouper."

"Wha'd I do?"

"Mommy told me how you tried to take Toddie to the library."

Maybe I'd done too good a job of acting. "Well, y'know, I'm a hockey player. You gotta play with pain. You can't let every little twinge stop you."

He kissed my nose. "That's my trouper." He stood up. "Okay, come on, we gotta hurry. Can you stand?"

"Hurry? Where're we going?"

"Hospital. C'mon, try standing."

"Oh no!" I screamed and dove under the covers and rolled myself into a ball in the corner of the bed.

"Come on, honey."

"No."

"Dimpus."

"No."

I could feel his hands all around me, trying to find a way through the covers. Something was making it. A finger. It reached my knee. I bit it. He howled. The finger left. "Megin, come out."

"I'm not going to the hospital just for a little cramp."

"Megin, you were having pain, weren't you?"

"So?"

"You were having so much pain you couldn't stand up, true?"

"I *was*. It's gone now."

"And do you know what you were pointing to when Mommy asked you to show her where the pain was coming from?"

"I don't know. My stomach or something."

"Your appendix."

"My appendix is fine."

"Let me tell you a story, Megin. A man at work, in floor coverings, Mr. Eckersley, has a daughter. Last year she had pains in that spot. They took her to the hospital. The doctor said she had acute appendicitis. He said if they had gotten her there a couple hours later, it might've been too late."

The jig was up — hospital or the truth. I took a deep breath: "I was faking it."

He laughed. He patted me where he probably thought my head was; actually it was my butt. "No, Dimpus, you weren't faking it. If Mommy thought you were faking it, she never would have called me. And if I thought you were faking it, I never would have rushed home from work. Especially when the man I was talking to wanted to buy two refrigerators."

What could I say? What could I do? I let him unwrap me, lead me downstairs, put my coat on me. Then he picked me up. "Daddy!"

"We have to be careful. The appendix can rupture."

"What's that mean?"

"Burst."

How embarrassing, my father carrying me out to the car like a baby. He kept muttering stuff like, "Trouper . . . gutsy little snapper . . ."

I didn't have appendicitis (surprise), so I was allowed to *walk* away from the hospital. Even so, as we were getting into the car, my father said, "Looks like you'll be staying in tomorrow, Dimpus."

"What do you mean?"

"You heard the doctor — 'Keep an eye on her for the next day or two.' "

"Daddy, they always say that. It doesn't mean I'm not allowed out."

"I think that's exactly what it means. Fasten your seat belt."

"Daddy, I don't *have* appendicitis. You heard him."

"I heard. And Mommy saw the pain you were in."

"I *can't* stay in tomorrow."

"No?"

"No. We have a game at the lake. We're playing the Skatium Rink Rats. I gotta be there."

"Fasten your seat belt."

"Daddy!"

"Fasten your seat belt."

When we got home and Grosso found out I wasn't allowed out next day, he didn't make a sound. But his grin was so wide that the ends of his mouth nearly knocked his ears off.

So I had to sneak out of the house next day. I listened for Grosso leaving for the game and waited as long as I could stand it. I went downstairs. Everybody was in the living room. "Am I allowed in the basement," I said, "or did the doctor say no basements?"

"By all means," chirped my father.

I had my hockey stuff stashed under the basement steps. In a couple minutes I was ready. I was inching the back door open when I heard a voice, Toddie's, behind me: "You can't go out."

I wheeled. "What're you doing here?"

"You can't go out. Daddy said. You sick."

I pressed my hand over his mouth. "Quiet. Shut up." I had to think. Fast. I knew my father would find out I was gone sooner or later, but I at least needed time to get to the lake. He wouldn't yank me off the ice. I thought about tying Toddie to the water heater and gagging him — I'd tell him it's a game — but I chickened out. There was no choice; I had to take him with me. "Toddie, wanna go see me play hockey?" He started yapping and hopping around. I had to muzzle him again. Luckily I found a ratty old coat of mine in the basement. It came down to his shoes. We took off.

By the time we got there, the first period was over. I pointed Toddie to the sideline and skated up to Skelley, who was in charge. "Who's winning?" I asked him.

"They are, one-nothin'." He wiped his nose on his sleeve. "Where you been?"

Grosso barged in from behind. "She's supposed to be home sick."

I smacked his stick. "Butt off, man."

"Sick?" said Skelley.

"I ain't sick. Look at me. Do I look sick?"

"Last night," went Grosso, "she had an attack of appendicitis. She couldn't even stand up."

"Butt out, I said!"

"My father had to take her to the hospital. Emergency room."

Skelley was staring at me. "Yeah?"

I laughed. "Skelley, do I look like I got appendicitis? Huh? Do I?"

Grosso wagged his stick at the sidelines. "There's Toddie. Go ask him. Ask him if I didn't have to take him to the library last night because she was having such terrible pains."

Ah, now I got it. Grosso was getting back at me for last night. "Skell," I said, "I was *faking* it. Y'know that Gretzky special on TV last night? I wanted to see it, so I pretended I was sick so I wouldn't have to take Toddie to the library."

Skelley's face was a blank.

"Yeah?" croaked Grosso. "Well listen, Skell, how come my father raced all the way home from work and took her to the hospital? Could she fake it *that* good?"

Silence. The whole team was standing around Skelley, gawking into his face. He wiped his nose on one sleeve, then on the other; looked like snails had been crawling over him. He looked back and forth from me to Grosso. He wiped his nose again. He looked down. He scraped ice with his skate blade till he had a little hill of snow. Then, real slow, he started shaking his head.

"What's that mean?" I said.

"It means no," quacked Grosso.

Suddenly I couldn't breathe. "Skelley?" He was still looking down, scraping ice. He mumbled something. I couldn't hear it. "What?"

"No."

"What do you mean by no? No *what*?"

Some Rink Rats came skating up, drumming sticks. "Yo! Let's go! Next period! You guys wanna forfeit?"

Skelley looked up. "Okay, let's go." The players started fanning out.

I grabbed his arm. "Skelley, no *what*?"

He was squinting at the sky. "You can't play."

"Skelley, I gotta! This is the big game! I gotta!"

Rink Rats laughed. "Go play with yer dolls!"

"Skell, we're losing! You *need* me!"

He pulled his arm away. "Come on, Megin, you gotta go." He headed out to center ice.

"Skell! I was *faking* it!"

"Fake yerself off the ice!" the Rink Rats were hooting. The Homesteaders were just standing, staring at me. Skelley stopped at the face-off spot. The Rink Rat center was waiting, and the referee. They just stood there, staring. The cold from below came seeping up through me. I shivered. I turned away and pushed off for the sidelines. My eyes were blurry. Somewhere ahead I saw Toddie, a face on top of my coat, grinning, holding something, something gleaming white and pink — the silly dressed-up egg Grosso had been carrying around all week. I reached out, I took the egg. I put the egg down on the ice. I nudged it with my stick. I looked up, at the players. No one was moving. It was all so blurry. The sun made sparklers in my eyes. I couldn't see faces. I couldn't tell one team from the other, only heard the Rink Rats hooting, louder and louder . . .

I wound up and blasted that egg to smithereens.

Greg

CAMILLE CAME TO ME flying and dying, her yellow blood streaking across the ice . . .

Megamouth didn't move, didn't try to get away, not when I pushed her into the snow, not when I grabbed her stick away. Poff was on me then, pinning my arms, but I was already moving off. I broke free and flung her precious Wayne Gretzky stick high over the slatted fence, out to the center of the lake. The stick cartwheeled headfirst into the thin ice and stuck there, upright, like the mast of a sunken boat.

I picked up the little pink-feeted pj's. Pieces of white shell were clinging. I laid it back in the box. I pulled the blanket all the way up.

"Don't play," Skelley kept saying, "you don't have to play." But I played. I don't know how good I was. I don't remember the score. I only know we lost.

When I left, the sun was setting like an egg yolk on the roof of Homestead House. All the way to Sara's, carrying the box, I kept forgetting I didn't have to be careful anymore.

Sara wasn't home. Nobody was home. I knocked and banged and rang the bell for five minutes. I went around to the back, checked the garages. I started to feel panicky. I had to find Sara, tell her, fast. Even though I knew she would be more upset about her grade than the egg.

I hung around for a while. Nobody showed up. Where could they be? Visiting? Out for dinner? I thought of leaving the box on the porch — but no, I had to be there. I went home. I started calling her house every fifteen minutes. If somebody answered, I would quick hang up and go over in person. Pretty soon I was calling every ten minutes. I couldn't eat. I kept looking at the little pink blanket. Where there used to be a nice little bulge, now was flat.

It was 10:20 before somebody picked up the phone. In ten minutes I was on her porch, ringing the bell. The porch light went on. Her father came to the door. He didn't say anything, just kept staring at the box.

"Mr. Bellamy? Could I see Sara a minute?"

He shook his left arm, brought his watch to his face, squinted, winced. "Little late, isn't it?"

"Yeah, I know. I'm sorry. But this is really important. It's about school. About our project for Health class. Something happened she has to know about."

He nodded at the box. "Is that the thing she's been walking around with?"

"Yeah, this is it. This is what I have to tell her about."

"Well, she's in bed."

"Already?"

He stiffened. "Tomorrow's a school day, son. Seems to me you coulda done this some other time."

Mrs. Bellamy's face appeared over his shoulder. "What's the problem?"

"Hi, Mrs. Bellamy."

She smiled. "You're Greg Tofer?"

I was surprised she knew me. "Yes, ma'am. Sorry to be here so late. Something happened —"

She looked at the box. She knew right then. "Oh no."

"I have to tell her."

She nodded with a small, pained smile and left the doorway. In a minute Sara was sliding past her father and stepping onto the porch. She wore a bathrobe and blue furry slippers. Her mother pulled her father inside and closed the door. The porch light went off.

Neither of us spoke. Sara kept staring at the box. Finally she reached in and pulled down the cover. She gasped and flipped it back up and went over to the steps. She looked out at the street, her back to me.

"What happened?" she said.

I told her.

"You should have let me keep it today."

"I was afraid to ask," I said. "Especially after turning you down when you wanted me to keep it."

"You should have asked."

"Would you have taken it?"

She answered with a shrug. Small fogs of breath passed from her dark silhouette into the street light. I said: "We almost made it. One day to go." She still said nothing. I moved to her side. Her eyes were closed, her lips tight together. Her cheeks were wet. I touched her. I traced one fingertip over the wetness, over her skin, from her eye to her lips. "Your face is cold," I whispered. "You look nice in your bathrobe."

Suddenly she was in my arms, sobbing, her face buried in my shoulder, the box clattering down the steps. "Jeez," I said, "I didn't know getting an A meant so much to you." She gave a squeak and kicked me in the leg and squeezed me tighter and cried even harder. Whenever it seemed like she was winding down, she started up again. I didn't know a girl could cry so much. Hey, Sara, I thought, an egg's an egg, remember? I was surprised she allowed herself to go on like that, but in a strange kind of way I was glad too. I just closed my eyes and held on.

How long were we standing there? I don't know. I only know that I opened my eyes and I saw the box overturned at the foot of the steps, one rocker off, and even though we were still squeezing each other, Sara wasn't crying anymore. Next thing I knew, I was kissing her. And *next* thing I knew, there were flashes all around. *Wow, so this is the fireworks you hear about!* Well, not quite — it was the porch light flashing on and off. I gave Sara another kiss, a quick one, and she reached for the doorknob. But before she went in, she poked her finger in my face and said, "Remember, I didn't ask you this time."

Megin

THE BIG TRIAL didn't start until Sunday night, late, in the living room. I sat on the sofa (electric chair). My father was pacing back and forth. The front door opened and Grosso came in with his silly pink box, but my father didn't notice, he just kept pacing. I thought he was going to cry, he looked so miserable.

"Man," I said, "all I did was break an egg. He can get a new one."

"I can't get a new one," Grosso spouted off. "It's too late. And even if it wasn't, I couldn't because the eggs were marked."

"Daddy, get him outta here," I said. Grosso was hanging in the dining room, like a vulture.

My father just stood there, slumpy, wagging his head. He looked in pain. His words came out creaking, like they needed oil. "See? Listen. It never stops. Fighting. Why? . . . Why?" He was looking at me, pleading. "*Why?*"

"Why what?" I said.

"Why can't you two get along? Why do you have to —"

He stopped, thunderstruck. "My God — look at your faces. Look at how you're looking at each other. Do you know what that look is? It's hate. Hate. Do you know that?"

Grosso shrugged.

I said, "So?"

"So?" he creaked. "So? A brother and sister that *hate* each other?" He started pacing again, creaking out the word, cocking his head like he was waiting for the word to talk back to him: "*hate . . . hate . . . hate . . .*" He stopped, turned to me, his hands outstretched. "*How . . . why . . . ?*"

"Daddy," I told him, "some things just are the way they are. Y'ever hear of the mongoose and the cobra? They hate each other. As soon as they see each other the first time. Natural enemies."

"But Megin," he said, "Gregory, you two used to get along fine."

"I don't remember," I said.

"Sure you did, sure you did." He broke into a huge smile. "When Greg was starting school, he used to teach you the alphabet on his little blackboard. I'll find it. I'll show it to you. And you, you used to cry when Greg left for school in the morning."

" 'Cause I was so happy."

"I gotta find that little blackboard."

"Anyway," I pointed out, "even if it's true, that was before he started putting his hairs in my toothbrush."

"And before she started putting roaches in my room," oinked Grosso.

"And before he threw away my hockey stick!"

"And before she killed my egg!"

"And before he got so ugly!"

"And before she got so grungy!"

"SHADDAAAAAPP!" My father stood in the middle

of the living room, arms spread out straight, head back, like he was waiting to be fitted for a cross. He stayed like that for a long time. Dead silence. Finally I couldn't stand it anymore. "Well, Daddy," I said, "you're always so jolly. But life isn't always jolly, you know."

First my father's head came down — now he looked like a scarecrow — then his arms, flopping to his sides. He took a deep breath. "Okay, here's the way we'll do it." He said I was grounded for the rest of the week, had to come right home after school, no later than 3:30. That wasn't all. Since my "beloved" hockey stick was gone, he said he would think about getting me a new one. *If.* If I obeyed the grounding rules, he would buy me a new one at the end of the week. But if I got home later than 3:30 on only one day, I wouldn't get a new stick till April.

"April!" I screeched. "The ice'll all be melted by then!"

He gave a wicked sneer. "That's about the size of it."

"Man, Dad, why don't you just chop my head off too while you're at it!"

"Good idea," honked Grosso.

"Okay," I said, "now what're you gonna do to *him?*"

"Never mind about him."

I didn't like the way he said that. "Hey — you're not gonna do anything to him, are you? I'm getting all the punishment and he's getting off free! Right?"

"That's my business."

"Yeah? Well then I'll make it *my* business to take care of him! My Wayne Gretzky stick is gone forever because of him, and if you think I'm not gonna make him pay for it, you're crazy!"

He turned on me like a wild dog. "Listen, young lady, *I'll* do the punishing around here, and right now you're the one who needs it most of all. I have to do something to put a stop to your rampage." He counted on his fingers. "You tricked your way out of taking Toddie to the library the other night. You pretended you were sick —"

"I didn't say I was *that* sick. *You* said I had appendicitis."

"Shut up. You pretended you were sick. You got me and Mommy all worried. I had to leave work, give up a big sale. You snuck out of the house yesterday. Against doctor's orders. You took Toddie with you, so we were worried sick not knowing where he was. And you ruined your brother's school project."

"And you're ugly," Grosso gonged in. My father hollered "Shut up!" at him, but by then the sofa pillow that I had thrown was already on its way. Grosso ducked and the pillow sailed into the dining room, over the table, and into the leaping leopard that my mother had made in ceramics class. The leopard leaped to the floor and crashed.

I didn't wait around. I was upstairs and in my room in two seconds. I buried my face in my pillow. It wasn't the crashing leopard that I kept seeing — it was my father's face, with a look that I had never seen before, a look that I knew not even my best dimple could wipe away, and I sank my teeth into my pillow knowing that my father, my very own father, hated me.

Greg

ON MONDAY I didn't have a good chance to talk to Sara until lunch. I spotted her coming through the cafeteria door and pulled her over by a window. It was starting to snow.

"Last time I touched you in school," I reminded her, "you slapped me."

She grinned. "Yeah, I know. Wha'd you think?"

"Ah, I don't know. First time I was ever slapped. Kinda shocked, I guess. I don't even think I felt it."

She pouted. "Oh phooey."

"Well, maybe I felt it a little."

"Still phooey."

"Well, now, come to think of it, I did feel a little dizzy afterward." We laughed. "So," I said, "how do *you* feel?"

"Me? Hm, let's see. How about decurioused?"

"Huh?"

"Well, I was always curious about what it's like to slap a man, like in the movies. Now I found out."

"Wha'd you find out?"

"I *like* it!" This time I caught her wrist as she was winding up. We laughed again, and I was thinking that no matter how long I lived, I would always remember Sara Bellamy as the first person who ever called me a man.

"Think it's gonna stick?" she said, looking out the window. The snow was falling pretty heavy now.

"Hope so," I said.

"Why?"

"So we get off."

"Go sledding?" There was a gleam in her eye. "Go chasing?"

I couldn't face her. I thought of her running after me up the hill, through the trees, her call getting fainter. "I'm sorry. That was rotten."

"*You* were rotten."

"*I* was rotten."

We both watched the falling snow. She sighed, "Well, I was probably a little moldy myself."

"No, not you."

"I shouldn't've been chasing you like that. I don't mean just up the hill either."

The snowflakes were fat, wet, the sticking kind. "Sara?"

"Mm?"

"What about, uh, Leo?"

"What about Leo?"

"I don't know. How come you went out with him?"

She ran her finger across the windowpane. "He asked me." She was grinning. "You think I went to him because of you, don't you?" I shrugged. "Well, you're right, I did. I wanted to see if he had any words of wisdom for a poor, innocent girl that some guy used as a stepping-stone to get to another girl."

"Did he?"

"Yeah. 'Wanna go to the mall with me?' "

We laughed. "I saw you that day," I told her.

"You did?"

"Yeah. I was on the upper level. I saw you and him going into the bookstore."

"Wha'd you think?"

"I wondered where you got that powder blue scarf and hat."

"What else? What did you feel?"

I didn't want to answer that. "Honest?"

She looked into my eyes. "Yes. Let's try honest from now on, okay?"

"Okay. I was relieved, sort of."

"Now that Leo got me off your back, you were free to go after Jennifer without having to feel guilty about me, right?"

I nodded. The fat, wet flakes were melting on the window ledge. "But I didn't feel relief when I saw you and Leo at the lake that time."

She laughed. "*Saw* us? You mean *crashed* into us. Boy, your little sister sure did a number on you that time."

"Yeah . . . well, the play was the worst."

"The school play? You were there?"

"Watching you every minute."

"You were?"

"Followed you into the lobby during intermission."

Her eyes were widening, present-opening eyes. "You did?"

"Went up to Valducci in the light room. Told him I couldn't stand it."

"Couldn't stand what?"

"You sitting there with Leo the Shrink. Were you holding hands?"

"None of your business. What else?"

"I walked the hallways. Heard somebody go into a room. Thought it was you and Leo."

"Yeah, what else?"

"Remember the end of the play? Lights flashing all around, swirling?"

"Yeah?"

"The spotlight was on you."

"It *was?*"

"You and Leo."

"Why?"

"Valducci was doing it. For me. So I could see you clearly, you and Leo."

In her eyes I saw that she had opened the present and that it was just what she had been hoping for. "Honest?" she said. I nodded. She looked out the window for a while, then turned to me. She fingered my sleeve. "When you ran up to see Valducci, what was it you said to him? Something about not standing it?"

"Yeah, well, that was it."

"No, *you* say it."

"I can't stand it."

"Anymore?"

"Yeah, anymore."

She tugged. "Okay now, say it again. Just like you said it to him. Just like."

I was starting to feel like an idiot. "Okay, uh — Valducci, I can't *stand* it anymore."

She didn't say anything more. The wide eyes were gone now. She just smiled, as though she had taken the present out and tried it on and found that it felt really good and fit perfectly. She kept smiling faintly as she turned to the falling snow, as we both turned and looked out at the falling, falling snow.

"It's sticking," I said.

"I know."

The bell rang. Kids were pushing out chairs, leaving. Sara and I looked at each other and broke out laughing: it had never occurred to us to eat.

After school I found a piece of paper in my locker, with writing on it. Looked like a poem, but it didn't rhyme. It said:

> *You were an egg.*
> *Or were you?*
> *You came into this world*
> *as an egg*
> *and you went out with a name*
> *and a warm place to lie down*
> *and a mother and father*
> *and love.*
> *They will remember you*
> *as Camille.*
> *You were an egg.*
> *Or were you?*

I met Sara out behind the school, by the bushes near the bike racks, as planned. I handed her the poem. "Did you write this?"

She read it, shaking her head. "No, but I think I know who did."

"Yeah? Who?"

"John Poff."

"Poff?"

"After sixth period, I thought I saw him slip something into your locker."

I couldn't believe it. "*The* John Poff? Football player? Weight lifter?"

"Him," she said, handing me the poem. I shook the snow from it, folded it, and put it in my pocket. I gave her the paper bag. "Shoot, I forgot to bring something to dig with."

"What are you going to use?"

"Hand, I guess." I looked around, picked a spot. "This okay?" She nodded. She was holding the bag close to her, with both hands. With my foot I cleared away snow; it was about three inches deep by now. I crouched, started digging. The ground was hard and cold. I thought my fingernails were ripping off. I just kept digging, clawing, until the tip of her boot touched my hand. "That's good enough," she said. One of my fingers was bleeding.

She crouched beside me. I took the bag from her. "Last look?" I said. She sniffed, nodded. I took out the little pink pj's, still with shell pieces clinging. A large snowflake landed on the *C* of *Camille*. It looked so pretty I didn't want to brush it away. We watched it melt, soak in. I put the pj's back in the bag, put Poff's poem in too, laid the bag in the hole, pushed the dirt back over, smoothed the ground.

We stayed there, watching the snowflakes land on the little plot, some melting, some not. "Well," I said, "did the experience speak to you?"

"It spoke," she sniffed, her voice raspy, "and it whispered and it hollered and it sang." She laid her hand on mine. "*Au revoir*, Camille."

Megin

I WAS too upset to eat breakfast. "Mom," I said, "why does he hate me?"

"He doesn't hate you."

"Then why is he doing this to me?"

"Because he's at his wit's end. He doesn't know what else to do. Eat your toast."

"I don't want any. But why does he have to ground me for a whole week? Right in the best part of hockey season. The ice is like a rock. Why can't I be grounded for a week in the summer? I'd take *two* weeks then."

"Misbehave now, pay the price later, huh?"

"Yeah, that's right."

"I don't think so. I think he needs a little satisfaction right now. Drink your juice."

"I'm not thirsty. Great. So I gotta suffer so he can get a little satisfaction. Wonderful father I got."

"You could've done worse."

"And what about my new stick? If I'm only one minute

late on one day, I don't get it till April. That's cruel. That's child abuse!" She laughed. "It's not funny!"

"I know. Sorry. Anyway, you can probably get away with being one or two minutes late." She pulled my juice over to her side.

"Are you gonna tell him if I'm late?"

She took a sip. "Won't have to."

"What do you mean?"

"He said he's going to call to make sure you're home."

I screeched and shuffleboarded my toast across the table. I stood up. "Mom, what about Emilie? How am I supposed to see her?"

"Well," she said, picking up the toast, "Beechwood Manor's on your way home from school. You'd have time to pop in and say hello for a second."

"But I don't *see* Emilie for just a second. And besides, I *never* go there without a french cruller — and by the time I went to Dunkin' Donuts and *then* to Emilie's and *then* home, I'd be so late I wouldn't get my new stick till the end of the *century.*"

She laid the toast down. "It's just a week. You'll survive. Emilie will wait. She'll understand. Let's just get it over with. Keep the peace."

I jammed the chair into the table. "Peace, bull!" I stormed out of the house. Halfway to school, my stomach was aching from hunger. I was glad.

I got home at 3:30 on the dot, just as my mother was opening her eyes on the sofa. Five minutes later the phone rang. She made me answer it. I picked up the receiver, snapped "The prisoner is present!" and bashed it down.

I got home on time Tuesday too, but it was getting harder. Usually I went to see Emilie early in the week,

Monday or Tuesday, and I knew she would start to wonder now. I went home a different way. I was afraid if I took my usual route past Beechwood Manor, Emilie might see me from her window. Or even worse, call to me. What could I say to her? "Sorry, Emilie, I'm not allowed to see you." "Sorry, Emilie, if I'm late I don't get my new hockey stick." "Sorry, Emilie, it's you or a new stick."

I felt rottener and rottener. At least she had her brother to come see her, I kept telling myself, even if he did make her stick to her diet. But she kept staring at me from her picture on my dresser. On Wednesday I ran home, blew in the door at 3:20. I couldn't stand being on the streets, thinking of Emilie, who was probably looking out her window, watching all the kids go by, wondering where I was, waiting, waiting. And probably, by now, figuring I'd never show up again. Typical teenager. Old people just a joke. Trade in an old hag for a new hockey stick any day.

She was probably starting to hate me by now. Well, why not? Join the crowd. My father hated me. Grosso hated me. I hated Grosso. In fact, come to think of it, I wasn't so crazy about myself. I was in bed, my room was dark, but still I could feel her eyes, her big, proud grin. Would she have traded me in for a new lacrosse stick? I got up and turned the picture toward the wall.

On Thursday after school I went straight to Dunkin' Donuts, paid for a half dozen french crullers (Jackie wasn't there), and took them to Beechwood Manor. As I walked through the lobby, the clock on the wall said 3:45. *Goodbye, hockey.* Emilie wasn't in her room, but somebody else was, an old hag. She was leaning on a cane and rooting through Emilie's dresser. I left her there gawking at me with her toothless mouth hanging open. I raced down to the lobby, to the man in the uniform at the desk. He was reading a magazine. "Somebody's in Emilie's room," I told him. "Emilie Bain. Room two-fourteen. She's robbing Emilie."

He put the magazine on the desk, but he kept reading it as he got up. "Come on!" I said. He took one last look at the magazine, turned it facedown, and started crawling toward the elevator. I grabbed his arm. "Stairs! Hurry!"

We made it in time. The hag was still there, her hand in a drawer, her toothless mouth gaping. "See?" I said. "See?"

The man asked the hag some questions. I couldn't understand her answers, with her lips flopping all over the place. When he asked her what her name was, it sounded to me like she said, "Buhbuhblubba Buhbuhblubba." Then he left.

"Aren't you gonna kick her out?" I said.

"She says it's her room."

"She's lying! It's Emilie Bain's!"

He shrugged. "I'll check the names."

"What's her name?" I asked him.

"Pendleton."

It started to hit me then that the room didn't look the same as before. I ran ahead, down to the lobby, into the office marked DIRECTOR — MRS. FLAGSTAFF. I practically crashed into her desk. "Where's Emilie Bain?"

She looked up. She blinked, smiled. She didn't seem to have any eyebrow hair, just two thin pencil lines. "Yes, dear?"

"Where's Emilie Bain?" She didn't answer. She just kept smiling, blinking, smiling, blinking. There was a green, cube-shaped soap eraser on her desk. I wanted to grab it and erase her stupid eyebrows. *"Where is Emilie Bain?"*

She jerked back, stopped blinking. The smile was gone. She came around the desk. She looked in pain. She put her hand on my shoulder. I twisted away from it, cringed back. "Where is she?" She was shaking her silly head. "What's that supposed to mean? Huh? Can'tcha talk?"

She closed her eyes, took a deep breath. "I'm afraid Emilie has passed away."

"Passed away? Waddaya mean, passed away?"

"She died, dear. Sunday afternoon. In her room."

I hated this lady. "No she didn't! There's nothing wrong with Emilie! We go racing down the hallway! I'm gonna teach her ice hockey!" Stick or no stick, we'll be out on the ice tomorrow, okay God?

"It happened in her sleep, dear."

She was heading for me again. I backed off. "Get away from me! Emilie's fine! She's here someplace! Did you tell her brother about this? Does he know what's going on?"

She pretended she didn't know what I was talking about. "Brother? Miss Bain had no brother. There were no living relatives."

No? Waddaya call me? "She has a brother!"

"Did you meet him, dear?"

"He comes to see her all the time! She sent him to get me a Gretzky T-shirt!" I ripped open my buttons to prove it. "Look!"

She was moving forward, coming after me, her pencil-line eyebrows wiggling like worms. "Sometimes, dear, we are lonely. Sometimes we invent others, even a brother, to keep us company." Suddenly she stopped, the eyebrows arched, she pointed. "Dear, is your name by any chance Megin?"

I backed into something, the lobby desk. The man in the uniform looked up from his magazine; he was starting to rise. I bolted for the door. "Something's going on here! Emilie! Emilie! Somebody's up there ransacking her room,

195

and you're saying she's not here, and you're saying she doesn't have a brother — Emilie! — and I'm going to the police! Y'hear!"

I burst through the door and I ran. I ran and I ran. I meant to go to the police, but I didn't. I didn't go home either. I just ran. And after a while I knew why I was running, exactly why. Jackrabbit chasers don't die, especially not in old folks' homes on Sunday afternoons, and jackrabbits — who ever heard of a jackrabbit that stopped running? I could see the critter up ahead of me, darting this way, that way, tail bobbing, flashing across the prairie — hah! look at it go! — but no way was it gonna get away, because I was a chaser now, but I knew that as long as I kept after it, chasing it, chasing it, everything would be okay, and Emilie would be waiting back in her room, room 214, and boy what a yip and holler she was gonna let out when she saw me stroll in holding that critter by the ears ... Then somewhere, somewhere after dark, the jackrabbit got away, and I knew then that everything the lady with the pencil-line eyebrows had said was true.

Greg

I DIDN'T WANT to sound like all of a sudden I was the big expert on how to get a girl, but I had to say something. After all, Valducci had helped me; now it was my turn to help him, even if the girl he wanted was a glittery seventh-grader from California. Anyway, ever since I saw her in a kimono on Megamouth's birthday, I've been thinking Valducci isn't so crazy after all. But there he was, as usual, chopping and high-kicking everything in sight on the way to school. I told him, "Valducci, you're not gonna get her that way."

"Ya-yagah!" He flicked a foot at Poff, his heel stopping an inch from Poff's nose. "Wha'd you say?"

"I said, you're not gonna get her that way."

"Who? What way?"

"Zoe. *That* way. Karate. Man of destruction."

He glowed at the mention of her name. "Zoe? You mean my honey? Fa-fa-*choo!*"

"I'm saying, Dooch, if you ever want her to *be* your honey, you better change your style."

"Oh, the big expert now, huh?"

"Dooch, I'm just trying to help ya."

"Yu-aaaahh-*hie!*" He chopped a small tree; all the ice coating its branches came tinkling down like it was suddenly undressed.

I pulled up my sleeve. "Look." He looked. "Notice anything?"

"You lost your tan."

"The vein, dumbo, remember my vein? How it humped up?"

"So?"

"So, it's gone. I haven't lifted a weight since last year. I stopped trying to be Mr. America, and I still got what I wanted."

"Who's trying to be Mr. America? Su-*su!*"

"I'm saying, you gotta be yourself."

"I am myself." He planted himself in front of Poff, contorted his body, and pulled his upper lip practically up to his eyes. "Foff, who av I?"

Poff broke out grinning.

"Dooch," I said, "you're not gonna get her that way."

"Get her? I already *got* her. Right where I want her. Any day now —" He spotted a dog taking a leak on a telephone pole. In no time at all the poor dog was on its butt, its one remaining hind leg cut out by a Valducci low-kick. The dog tore off.

"Any day now what?" I asked him when I stopped laughing.

"Any day now — pah-*pah!* — she's gonna ask me out — *yonga!*"

We were at school by now, and sure enough, he spotted Zoe. She was with some other girls. They were taking turns putting an apple on their heads and seeing how far they could walk without it falling off. When Zoe got the apple and put it on her head, Valducci moved in. Oh no! I thought. Give Valducci credit — he didn't do it from behind. He jumped right in front of her, squatting. She stopped, froze; he twirled sideways, up shot his leg — he looked like the dog taking a leak — "Fu-*chaya!*" Into the air popped the apple; it landed ten feet away in the snow. Valducci bowed, turned, and strutted into school. Some of the girls started howling with laughter, and some of them just looked at Zoe, who was not laughing at all.

When I saw Valducci in gym class, he went thumbs up: "Any *minute* now."

At lunchtime: "Any *second* now."

Then, after school, who came straight for us but Zoe, and my first thought was, Either he's right, or she's gonna kick him. Neither. She came to me. "Megin sick?" she said.

"I don't know," I told her. "I don't keep track of her."

She gave me a good glare — a California glare, I guess; then she snapped away so fast her dangling earrings went flying out flat after her.

Two minutes later, Megamouth's pal Sue Ann came running. "Is Megin sick?" I told her the same thing.

Valducci and I split, went home, and met at the lake. We were right in the middle of some one-on-one when I heard somebody screeching my name from the sidelines. Sue Ann again. I yelled for her to wait but she kept screaming. I went over. She was gasping, her face was bright red, tears were rolling down her cheeks. "Go home! Fast! Your mom called! Megin! Fast!"

I was up to the street before I realized I still had my

skates on. I turned to go back for my sneakers and bumped into Sue Ann. She was holding them.

A police car was parked in front of our house. Little kids stood across the street, sled ropes in their hands. Eyes, faces jerked toward me when I opened the door, and for a second it seemed like I had barged in on a picture just ready to be taken: my mother on one end of the sofa; the policeman on the other, note pad, pencil in hand; Toddie clinging to my mother, crying; my mother's eyes so open, like they get when she's coming out of her trance, only red now; standing behind the sofa, Zoe, little black streaks creeping down from her eyes; a stack of schoolbooks on the coffee table.

All eyes came talking through my mother's voice: "Do you know where Megin is?" My mouth wouldn't work. I shook my head. "Don't you know anything? *Anything?*"

"What's there to know?" I said. "She went to school, didn't she?"

My mother's eyes fell to the books on the coffee table. She seemed hypnotized.

"Her books were found along West Chester Pike," came the calm, ministerlike voice of the policeman. "You didn't see her on the way to school?"

"No. She usually leaves before me."

A knock on the door. I opened it. Sue Ann came in, took a look at the books, then at my mother, and burst out bawling. Before I could shut the door, my father was barging in. He stared at the books too, and next thing I knew he was hugging me and practically squeezing my breath out.

The books were found by a man who runs a rug store on West Chester Pike. There are a lot of businesses along there. It's a busy highway a couple miles from our house. The policeman kept saying there was probably nothing to worry about, probably nothing bad had happened to her. He said kids do this all the time, play hooky, disappear for a couple hours, worry their parents sick. They always show up by night. That's why the police don't list somebody as missing until they're gone for twenty-four hours.

Night came, but not Megin.

Megin

I WAS halfway to school when it hit me: Emilie was dead, my Wayne Gretzky stick was gone, I was through playing hockey, everybody hated me — so what was I doing going to *school?* I turned off at the next street.

I wound up at Dunkin' Donuts. I never saw it so crowded, every seat at the counter taken. Jackie looked at me, then the clock. "Don't you have school?" I told her some lie about not having to be there till eleven. She took me into the back and stuffed me with blueberry-filleds. Warm blueberry-filleds. I was sorry I couldn't act more grateful. I was tired; I hadn't slept good. In the soft sizzle and squish of the donut-making room, I felt like I was floating in a warm, sweet dream cloud. Then Jackie took out a pan of french crullers. I couldn't look. I zippered up my jacket, grabbed my books. Jackie called as I was heading out: "Moxie — you forgot." She was holding out a cruller. I didn't know how to say no. She wrapped it in a napkin and handed it to me, and for the first time, I thought

I felt crying coming on. But it didn't. I stuffed the donut in my pocket and left.

I headed for the nearest snow bank and started kicking my way along it. You scum! You rat! You murderer! You killed her! She was on a diet and you kept feeding her french crullers! Smuggling them to her week after week! Till you killed her! I took out the cruller and winged it; it exploded against the side of a car going by. "You stupid, stinking, rotten, scummy murderer kid!"

I was sorry I'd eaten. Rotten kid, stuffing yourself with warm donuts, your own stinking favorite warm donuts, while your friend — *your grandmother!* — lies dead in the ground. I punched and punched my books into my stomach until I threw up, blueberry-filled, even warmer now, all over the snow.

I felt better. I felt worse.

I walked. I saw a squirrel scamper across a telephone wire. I tried to imagine myself catching a squirrel. Impossible. I never knew anyone who caught one. Or even *tried* to catch one. Or even *thought* about trying to catch one. And if anybody ever did, with their bare hands, who would believe them?

I came to West Chester Pike. I had walked there a couple times with Sue Ann, to look at stores, but never by myself. I looked down the road. Nothing but stores, gas stations, eating places on both sides. I knew that some ways out there they came to an end with a Seafood Shanty. Then there were things like funeral homes and apartment houses and golf courses and farms. And it got hilly out there. I could see the hills from where I stood. That was the West. North Dakota was west, out west somewhere, out beyond those hills. The prairie. And, maybe, a jackrabbit waiting. I put down my books and headed west.

I always heard that your whole life passes before you if you're drowning. I think it also happens if you're walking west. Things came to me that I never knew were still in my head. My father was right; my brother did give me lessons on a little blackboard, and I did cry when he went off to school. But there was also the time I locked him in a closet and tried to suck all the air out with a straw.

I sort of ran through my life from beginning to end — or present, that is. I zipped through the last week in a couple seconds. Then I went back and did the highlights in slow motion: the time I got my autographed Gretzky stick, the donut fight in the kitchen, the time Toddie barfed in the cider vat, the time I asked Emilie to be my grandmother. Emilie was waiting at the end of each memory, in her room, on Sunday afternoon, alone. Or was she? If she really did make up a brother to give herself company, like the lady said, maybe, in her imagination, he was with her then. I hoped so, for her sake, so she didn't have to die alone. But I felt bad about that too, because if she had to invent a brother, that meant having me wasn't enough. And why a brother? I figured if I was an old lady and I was lonely, the last kind of person I'd invent to keep me company would be a brother.

When I finally took a break from thinking and remembering, I didn't know where I was. The stores were gone. I looked back. The big boat on the Seafood Shanty sign was barely visible in the distance. I must have walked for miles. I wondered what time it was. Probably around lunch. Sue Ann would be wondering where I was. She wouldn't have anybody to ask, because she knows that when I'm not going to school, she's the one I tell. I knew what would happen. As soon as school let out, she would go to my house. I could picture her going to pieces when she found out I wasn't there either. Good old Sue Ann.

I turned back.

Somewhere along the way, I left the pike, and a long time later I came wandering up to a big, long, brownstone building. It was the Homestead House. I wasn't used to seeing it from this direction. The lake was out in front. Kids were skating. Must be after school, I thought.

I checked the back door. Locked. Not surprising, since the House is only open on weekends during the winter. Just for the heck of it I tried a window — it came open. I climbed in. I was in the kitchen. Big old wooden table. Fireplace big enough for me to walk into. Big black pots. Bunches of dry plants and weedy-looking stuff hanging from a beam. On the table was a jar of something, big jar. Dried apples. I ate them all.

I went upstairs. Steep, narrow, creaky. Maybe scary too, but I was too tired to be scared. Dead tired. I went into a room, a bedroom. Besides the bed, nothing but an old wooden chest, a table with a bowl and pitcher, and a rug that looked like it was braided with string. I looked out the window. I could see my stick jutting out of the ice in the middle of the lake. Somebody was running up the hill. Looked like Grosso. I lay down on the bed. The mattress was lumpy and crinkly, but I didn't care. I reached out to the floor and dragged up the stringy rug. I folded it in half and curled myself under it and went to sleep.

Greg

I DIDN'T NEED my skates. Or my gloves or kneepads or any of the other fancy stuff. Just my stick and puck. And darkness. And the practice board. Last time I was at the lake knocking the puck into the board, I was trying to figure out Jennifer Wade. I'd never in a million years thought my sister would ever be the reason for me being there.

The cop hadn't fooled me. I knew what had happened. Oh sure, she probably was just playing hooky at first. So she went out to West Chester Pike, walked along it. Then she decided to thumb a ride, run away, really show everybody she wasn't kidding. So a car stops, picks her up. She's already in the car before she realizes he's a creep, and even she knows what happens to girls that get picked up by creeps. She tells him to stop the car, she wants to get out. He laughs, just laughs, and reaches over and grabs her. She opens the door, tries to get out, he won't let her, she throws her books out, they land in front of the rug store, the car speeds off up the pike, the door swinging shut ... And then, a couple days later, we meet. At the mall, the mall parking lot. He's got her locked in a van. I see her face at the back window, silently calling, "Greg! Help me!" And there he is, coming out of the mall, with food, two pizzas. I kick the pizza boxes out of his hands (I'm Valducci). Another kick under the chin lifts him three feet off the ground. I snare him on the way down and sling him (I'm Poff) into the side of the van, and then as he crumples I'm pounding and kicking him and I'm all me and I'm kicking and kicking into the face that's crying and begging for mercy, kicking, kicking . . . only for real, for cold ice real, it's not my foot smashing his face to a pulp, but my stick smashing the puck into the board, and it's not him crying, but me.

I thought about the donut fight in the kitchen. I thought about the time she locked me in a closet and tried to suck the air out with a straw. I laughed. Then I thought about the schoolbooks on the coffee table. It was my fault, no getting around it. There was nothing in the world she loved more than that hockey stick personally autographed by Wayne Gretzky. Nothing. If she still had her stick, she probably would never have taken off. But she didn't have it. Because of me. And now I wasn't even sure why I threw it away. Was it really because she smashed Camille? Or was it because she was the one, not me, who'd had the winning ticket number at the hockey game that night?

I turned and wound up and sent the puck across the lake. It shot out of sight, into the darkness. I heard it knock against the slatted fence, sending the whole thing into rattles. As it turned out, the darkness wasn't so bad after all. By the time I got within five feet of the fence, I could see it fine. It was easy enough to climb over; they sure didn't put it there to block people who really wanted to get to the other side. I stomped a couple times — the ice was firm. I couldn't see the stick yet, but I knew about where it was. I moved out, slowly, sideways, arms out, ready to jump back at the first crack, the faintest crinkle. But the ice was solid, like a rock. Which figured. The last couple days the temperature never got much above twenty. In fact, looking at the stick that afternoon, I thought I noticed it jutting up a little higher, which would happen, thickening ice pushing it up. I crouched low, trying to place the stick against the distant, dim light of the street. Still couldn't see it. I moved on. Sideways. Slow. Then — there it was, right in front of me, I had almost gone past it. Slow, slow, a couple steps, little steps — *Don't blow it now* — reach — reach — I had it.

Megin

AT FIRST when I woke up I thought there was a slow-moving clock somewhere in the house: *tock–tock–tock*. But no, it was coming from outside. I got up and went to the window. The floodlights were out; must've been after nine. From the street a faint light smudged the hockey-playing end of the lake. I could see a dark figure, near the practice board: *tock–tock*. Then I knew: El Grosso. One of his weird habits. When something is bothering him, he goes to the lake and shoots his puck into the board. Probably still trying to figure out how to get Jennifer Wade.

Then, suddenly, fear hit me, like a hot puck into my stomach. I was scared of being in this old, dark, cold house by myself, and just as scared of what was going to happen when I got home. I headed for the door, felt my way along the hallway, down the narrow, creaky stairs, pitch-black now, like the House of Horrors at the shore. I expected a green ghoul or headless mummy to come popping out at me any second. I made it to the kitchen. Silence, inside and out: the *tock–tock* had stopped. I swore I felt ghoul's breath on the back of my neck. I bumped into the table, found the door, I fumbled around, yanked, pulled, but I couldn't open it. I went out the way I came in, through the window. I was in such a hurry I snagged my foot and fell to the ground on my head.

Just as I got up and started to run I heard a voice — from the lake — Grosso — calling for help! In a couple seconds I was on the ice. I stopped, listened: silence. I called his name. "Over here! Over here!" His voice was coming from the middle of the lake, the *thin ice!*

I started running, slipped, slid all the way into the fence. I kicked it down, stepped over it, stopped. Now I could hear: splitting ice, splashing . . .

"Greg?"

"Here! Here!"

I was there. He was a dark thrashing shape that the blacker darkness was trying to swallow. I could hear more than see: gasping, wheezing, like his lungs were rusty springs, grunting, blubbing, smacking water, smacking ice, ice snapping. *Your brother is drowning.* I reached out. "Stop!" he yelled. "No!" Ice collapsed, he disappeared. He came back up, farther away, glubbing, his breath singing. *Your brother is dying.* I tore off my coat, got on my knees, held the coat by one cuff, tossed it into the black water. "Here! Grab!"

He thrashed his way over. "No! Here!" he gasped. For the first time, I noticed he was holding something; it looked like a hockey stick. "Back!" he gasped. "Back! Back!" I crawled back. "Sit!" I sat. "Dig! Heels in!" I dug my heels in as well as I could. He shoved the stick at me. It *was* a hockey stick, and as soon as I grabbed it I knew exactly which one it was. The stick between us seemed a mile long. At the other end I could barely see his eyes. They were scared. I took a deep breath and pulled.

Greg

AT THE OTHER END of the stick, for a split second, I saw her eyes. They were scared. Then she grunted and pulled, I was coming forward, and then the ice in front of her, the ice around her, was cracking, was gashing open with a noise like fresh apples splitting, and she sank, still sitting, still pulling, still scared eyes. We sank together, the stick stiff between us, connecting us. We hit bottom, then, suddenly, the other end of the stick popped up, the weight gone from it. I pushed off the bottom, broke water. "Megin! Megin!" I jerked around — nothing, silence. I gulped air, dove. Underwater, black water, I swept the stick back and forth, back and foth, sweeping, sweeping — *Hit somebody! God please hit somebody!* — sweeping, sweeping all the black cold waters of the world, *please, please,* and I saw her face before me, blueberry filling smearing her cheeks and nose, lemon in her hair, laughing laughing, then my breath was gone and I had to find more — *fast!* I pushed upward, but instead of breaking water I smashed into something — ice. I was under the ice! With the butt-end of the stick I started ramming the ice. My lungs demanded something, if not air, water. *You are drowning. You and your sister are drowning together*. Ram! Ram! Ram! I broke through, shot up shedding ice and gorged myself on air. "Megin! Megin!" Something thumped me from behind: Megin, grasping, gasping. I lifted the stick clear of the water and heaved it as far as I could, back to the days when the sun flashed from our skate blades and we skimmed over ice bright and hard as diamonds. I tried to grab her with my hand, but my frozen fingers wouldn't close. I clamped my arm around her waist, she did the same to me, and we started paddling with our free arms, kicking, thrashing, straining for the ice. When we reached it and leaned on it, it broke. We started over. I don't know how many times we did it — paddling, clinging, leaning, sinking — I only know that all of a sudden we weren't sinking anymore, it was solid beneath us, *solid*, the ice was holding, we were out!

That's when I found out how cold I really was. I wasn't shivering, I wasn't trembling — I was slamming, in all directions at once, like some machine loose on its bolts. My body was all on its own, I couldn't make it do anything for me. But that was okay, because I didn't really want much now anyhow, just one of two things: either a nice, hot, steamy shower (which was impossible) or to die, that's all, before another second went by. But somebody was pulling at me, Megin, pulling at me, saying things, and we were moving, up the hill, my body slamming, Megin saying things, cold, slamming, slamming ... then steps, lights, voices ... "Joan! C'mere! Quick!" ... hands, dry, blankets, slamming, cold ... "Okay, careful now, easy does it, lift — lift" ... car, lights, too bright, voices, cold, hands, voices, cold, voices voices voices ...

Megin

THE NURSE was bringing my second cup of hot tea when Toddie and my parents came in. My mother and Toddie had a race to my bed. My mother won. She grabbed me and hugged me and broke out bawling. With my mother smothering my head and Toddie taking over my middle, my father got what was left — my feet. He hugged them and started sniveling away. That got me started. By the time the rest of them were cried out, I was still going full blast. My mother was stroking my hair and begging me to stop. She kept asking me if I had been abducted. When I could finally speak, I said, "What's abducted?"

"Kidnapped," she sniveled.

"*Kidnapped?*"

"Yes. Were you?"

Suddenly I remembered. "How's Greg?"

She smiled, wiping my tears. "He's going to be all right, the doctor said. Close call."

"He was blue. He couldn't move."

"He was in the water for a long time. Another couple minutes —" She started crying again. "He said . . . said you saved him."

I shrugged. "I don't know who saved who."

She kissed me and hugged me some more. My father cradled my feet on his lap and squeezed them through the blankets.

"Now," my mother sniffed, *"were* you abducted? Kidnapped?"

"You mean did somebody snatch me?"

"Yes. Well?"

"Why would anybody wanna snatch *me?*"

"Megin. Just *did* they?"

"Did who? Who's *they?*"

"*Anybody!* Snatch you?"

I laughed. "Jeez no!" And she grabbed me again and we cried some more.

Toddie reached for the hot tea and gave me his pleading face. "Sip?"

"A sip," I said.

Then they started asking me a million questions, but I was saved by the nurse. She told them I needed rest. She almost had to kick them out. Then, for the second time that day, I went to sleep in a bed that wasn't my own.

When they came next day, they brought something with them.

"My stick!"

"It was found on the ice," my father said, bowing and presenting it to me. I hugged it, I kissed it. "Seems like you two made the lake a tourist attraction. There's a whole crowd down there looking at the big hole in the ice. You're famous."

"And something from Jackie at Dunkin' Donuts," said my mother, handing me a pink-and-purple box. It was crammed with blueberry-filleds. My mother pushed my hand away, took one out, gave it to me, and closed the box. "Sue Ann and Zoe send their love and say hello."

Then she handed me another box, wrapped in Christmas paper. I tore it open. It was something to wear, knitted, red. I took it out: a sweater. There was a little white envelope. It said, "For Megin." I opened it.

> *I told you I can't knit!!*
> *Love,*
> *Your Grandmother*

She was right. One sleeve was longer than the other, and the whole thing was sort of cockeyed. I couldn't talk, couldn't see very well either.

"The director from Beechwood Manor brought it this morning," my mother was saying. "She found it in Emilie's room. It wasn't wrapped yet. She read the card, saw the name. That's all she had to go on. She said a girl came in Thursday afternoon—" She kissed me on the forehead. "That was you, wasn't it?" I nodded. "She called the junior-high office. It's a good thing we named you Megin. There's only one Megin in the school. They gave her our address." I was clutching the sweater, crying into it. "I was very, very sorry to hear about Emilie."

After a while she lifted my face and dried my eyes and smiled. "Let's go."

"Where?"

"Home."

"Now?"

"Doctor says you're okay."

"What about Greg?"

"One more day for him."

I pulled the curtain around the bed and got dressed. My father kept saying, "I see your fee-eet." I put my new sweater on. Besides everything else, it was about ten sizes too big.

On the way down the hall, my father said, "There's Greg's room." They stopped and looked at me. I took a deep breath and went in. Somebody else was there, a girl with a light blue scarf. She was leaning over the bed so I couldn't even see him. I left. "He's busy," I said, and we went home.

Greg

USUALLY I don't like a big fuss on my birthday, but since it came just two days after I got out of the hospital, my mother said we should make it into a welcome-home celebration. I was arguing with her and telling her no, forget it, when I happened to notice the situation: it was 3:15 in the afternoon, but my mother was not in the living room lying on the sofa. She was in the kitchen, her hands were flipping through cake recipes, her mouth was telling me how to celebrate my birthday, and her eyes were wide open. She was not surviving.

"Okay," I said, "if it's a little celebration."

So I invited Sara and Poff and Valducci. Then I told Megin she could invite friends of hers. I knew she would ask Sue Ann and Zoe. I didn't tell Valducci.

Poff and Valducci were the first to arrive. We were in the basement shooting darts when the doorbell rang, and Valducci, at the sound of Zoe's voice, kangarooed up the steps, dart in hand. A few seconds later there was a howl. Poff and I ran upstairs. Toddie, scowling, fierce, was pushing

Valducci across the living room, away from Zoe. Valducci backed into the wall. He looked at us, shocked. "He *kicked* me."

"Zoe *my* girlfrenn," Toddie snarled and kicked him again.

Give Valducci credit. A couple minutes later he came up with something that even Toddie approved of. He got an apple from my mother. He held his dart out to Zoe and said, "Miss Miranda, I besmirched your honor and ruined your apple last week at school. Now, you may take your revenge." Zoe just stood there staring, so Valducci put the dart in her hand. Then he backed up about five feet and stood at attention and placed the apple on his head. "Fire when ready," he said.

Only Toddie made a sound ("Shoot, Zoe, shoot!"). Everybody else was just gaping. As well as I know Valducci, even I didn't know if he was serious, and I could tell by the faces that nobody else knew either. Zoe stared at him for a long while. You could see her thinking about all the times he'd pestered her; and the more she thought, the faster the dart rolled in her fingers. Then her face changed, just a little, and her hand was rising, up to her shoulder, then pulling back; her eyes were narrow, her lips tight. Sara grabbed my arm. My father reached out — "Okay now —" but his words were cut short by Zoe's arm snapping forward and all eyes shot to the apple — and then Zoe was laughing, and her hand was hanging limp at her side, still holding the dart.

She was still laughing when she walked over to Valducci, still stiff at attention, and took the apple from his head. She took a bite of it, not laughing now, looking right into his eyes, the way you'd never see a seventh-grader do to a ninth-grader, and I knew she had seen the same thing I had seen: that Valducci had never flinched, not even when the dart was snapping forward. His eyes never blinked, the apple never moved. Sorry, Toddie, I thought, you lost.

I'd never heard "Happy Birthday" sung so loud before. Usually it was just my mother and father and Toddie. I was embarrassed. I kept staring at the candles on the cake. I couldn't wait for them to finish the song. Then a funny thing happened:

> "Happy birthday dear Gre-eg,
> Happy birthday —"

Right in the middle of the final line, the singing stopped. I looked up. Sara was grinning. They were all grinning at me. Then they all turned to the other end of the table, and my sister, her face in candle glow, swamped in her new red sweater that fit her like a bathrobe, my sister Megin, sang the rest all by herself: "tooooo you."